BAD GIRLS

BAD GIRLS

CAMILA SOSA VILLADA

Translated from the Spanish by Kit Maude

OTHER PRESS / NEW YORK

First softcover edition 2024
ISBN 978-1-63542-440-9

Originally published in Spanish as *Las malas* in 2019
by Tusquets Editores S.A., Buenos Aires
Copyright © 2019, Camila Sosa Villada
Copyright © 2019, Tusquets Editores S.A.
2020 Latin American Rights Agency – Grupo Planeta
English translation copyright © 2022, Kit Maude

Production editor: Yvonne E. Cárdenas
Text designer: Jennifer Daddio / Bookmark Design & Media Inc.
This book was set in Filosofia and Flood by
Alpha Design & Composition of Pittsfield, NH

1 3 5 7 9 10 8 6 4 2

Library of Congress Cataloging-in-Publication Data
Names: Sosa Villada, Camila, author. | Maude, Kit, translator.
Title: Bad girls / Camila Sosa Villada ; translated from the Spanish by Kit Maude.
Other titles: Malas. English
Description: New York : Other Press, [2022]
Identifiers: LCCN 2021047588 (print) | LCCN 2021047589 (ebook) |
ISBN 9781635422023 (hardcover) | ISBN 9781635422030 (ebook)
Subjects: LCGFT: Fiction.
Classification: LCC PQ7798.429.O757 M3513 2022 (print) | LCC PQ7798.429.O757 (ebook) |
DDC 863/.7—dc23/eng/20211019
LC record available at https://lccn.loc.gov/2021047588
LC ebook record available at https://lccn.loc.gov/2021047589

FOR

CLAUDIA HUERGO

AND

CARLOS QUINTEROS

We were all to be queens.

—GABRIELA MISTRAL

The Word *Travesti*

Down below the equator, right at the end of the world, we banded together to dig up the word *travesti*. It had been decorously buried under terms that were completely alien to us. People were calling us trans women, transsexuals, or transgender, and even mentioned conditions such as gender dysphoria and sexual dissidence. Once again Northern academia was being thrust upon us while down here we were busy surviving, living, fucking, and eating, even if all there was on our plates was dirt. They developed theories about us to make our existence more hygienic because they couldn't stand letting something go unexplained. We, the Latin American travestis, sculpted by the hands of all those who went before, knew what we were, unaware that we'd be buried beneath a stony avalanche of identity. Or something else just as deadly.

I don't know who was the first to start looking. Soon the oldest among us were urging others to join the dig. We found the word travesti underneath layers of first-world theory, piles and piles of books on medicine, psychiatry, and psychology, underneath poetics that never came close to our mysteries. Theirs was a form of assimilation that sought to establish different levels of commitment to the travesti experience—which and how many operations had been performed on a body, what hormonal treatments had been applied, varying dreams of public and private lives, whether the penis had been kept or not, what a body wanted and rejected. It was like listening to someone who knew nothing about us gossip about our lives. But we knew that a better word lay intact underneath all the screed.

In the cemetery where one finds so many anonymous travestis, many of whom only linger in the memory as a nickname or famous deed, down where roots glow phosphorescent, something of their existence still pulses with life. We removed the upper layers of theory and what was left were the insults, covered very nicely in good manners and prudish, white politesse. The insults did feel familiar, so we removed them carefully. Far below, where the secret rivers of the world flow, appeared a word that stank of death, shit, semen, prostitution, the night, the cold, bribery, blood and jail, of misery and neglect. A word sharp as a knife, grime-encrusted and wounding. A word that spoke not just of the creatures we were and are but also of our poverty, of the acts that made us legendary, of the courage with which we headed out to live among families and communities. We didn't want to look like women, we didn't want to hide our struggles in any way, we didn't feel trapped in the wrong bodies, we didn't know what we were doing. But in the street, they christened us with that old, buried word, highlighting our beauty, which was like a home. *¡Travesti!* they cried, and it was enough to conjure an image, the rejection of a whole society wedded to a form of identification. To them, calling us travestis was a way of insulting us. But we weren't strangers. We were already here, the same as you, and had been for a very long time. The abundance of these lands belonged to us too.

And so, I don't use the term trans women, I don't use surgical vocabulary, cold as a scalpel, because the terminology doesn't reflect our experience as travestis in these regions, from indigenous times to this nonsense of a civilization. I reclaim the stonings and spittings, I reclaim the scorn. You may ask how it can be that a writer proudly identifies herself with an insult. My answer is that you're looking for the way out up there, where you think your thoughts are formed. So elevated, useful, and precise. We, after years and years of holding back the travails of Latin America with our bodies, know that you have to delve deep, go down, learn from other creatures who treasure their ignorance of themselves. We know it's better to escape through tunnels than try to leap over walls.

Las malas, the "bad girls," are travestis, and even in their worst moments they wouldn't want to go by any other name.

BAD GIRLS

THE NIGHT AIR in the Park is dense, dark, and freezing. The ancient trees, recently stripped of their leaves, look askance to the heavens, pleading for some obscure boon essential to vegetation. A group of *travestis* makes its rounds in the shadows cast by the branches. They almost seem to move as one body, cells from the same animal, or members of a pack. Potential johns cruise by in their cars, slowing down to inspect the group before selecting one with the wave of an arm. The chosen woman answers their call. Night after night, nothing changes.

Sarmiento Park is right in the heart of the city. A large green lung with a zoo and a theme park. At night it turns wild. The travestis wait in the shelter of the branches or by the side of the road, casting their spell from the jaws of the wolf that stands next to the statue of Dante, who also lends his name to the avenue. Every night, the travestis drag themselves out of a hell that no one would ever think to write about, to bring spring back to the world.

With them is a pregnant woman, the only one of them to have been born female. The rest, the travestis, have worked their own transformation. Among the fellowship of travestis of the Park, she's different, the pregnant woman who always plays the same joke. grabbing an unwitting travesti's crotch as though to catch her out. She reaches for one now and they all laugh.

The caravan of travestis isn't fazed by the cold. A hip flask of whiskey is passed from hand to hand, scraps of folded paper filled with cocaine go from nose to nose, some of which are large and natural, others cut down to size by the surgeon's scalpel. The devil lends what nature has withheld. In the Park that borders the center of the city, the seductive allure of travesti bodies emanates from pits of damnation. Auntie Encarna joins in the sabbath with ferocious enthusiasm. The cocaine has given her a boost. She's one of the eternals, invulnerable as an ancient stone idol. But something out there, in the depths of the cold night, attracts her attention, drawing her away from her friends. Something is calling to her from the darkness. As mouths embellished with lipstick cackle and ingest the whiskey and cars honk in search of a moment's happiness with a travesti, Auntie Encarna makes out a very different sound indeed, a sound made by someone not at all like the cast of characters to whom we've been introduced so far.

The other travestis continue on their way, ignoring Encarna. Auntie has been a little scatterbrained lately. There comes a time in everyone's life when their memory isn't what it used to be. To keep up, she's taken to writing everything down in notebooks and sticking notes to the refrigerator. Some think she's going crazy, others that she's grown weary of remembering. Auntie Encarna has suffered more than her fair share of beatings; boots belonging to policemen and tricks alike have danced plenty of jigs on her head and kidneys. The latter organs are now so badly damaged that she pees blood. So no one pays any attention when she goes off, leaving them behind, answering the siren call of fate. She wanders away, a little disoriented, treading painfully in acrylic shoes that at 178 years of age make her feel as though she's walking on a bed of nails. She hobbles through the dry earth and weeds that grow in the neglected regions of the Park, careering across Dante Avenue like a wolf whistle, into an area full of brambles, hillocks, and a cave where faggots seek out lips and reassurance, now known as the Bears' Grotto. A few feet farther on is Rawson Hospital, where infections are seen to: our second home. Ditches, emptiness, thorn bushes, masturbating drunks. While Auntie Encarna disappears into the thickets, the magic begins to happen. Whores, horny customers, chance hookups in an improvised forest, everyone giving and receiving pleasure in cars parked askew, lying among the weeds, or up against a tree. This is the hour when the Park becomes a pleasure womb, a recipient for sex with no shame attached. There's no telling whose hands and tongues belong to whom. Right now, in this place, couples are fucking. But Auntie Encarna is on the hunt for a voice, or scent maybe. You never know when she's going to go off sniffing for something. She gradually begins to realize what she's looking for: a crying baby. Auntie Encarna feels through the darkness with her shoes in hand, plunging farther into the inhospitable undergrowth, determined to see it with her own eyes. Hunger and thirst. The baby's cries are full of them and in response Auntie Encarna desperately quickens her pace: somewhere in the forest a child is suffering. It's winter in the Park, cold enough to freeze your tears.

Encarna eventually finds him by the drainage ditches where the whores hide from police cruisers. The child is covered in prickly branches, wailing desperately. It feels as though the Park is crying with him. Auntie Encarna is frantic, the horror of the world presses down on her throat.

The boy is swaddled in an adult coat, a green puffer jacket. His bald head makes him look like a parrot. She gets scratched as she reaches down to rescue the child from his tomb of thorns. Her skin starts to bleed, staining the cuffs of her blouse. She looks like a veterinary midwife shoving her hands into a mare to pull out a foal. She feels no pain, doesn't even notice the cuts. She keeps pulling away the brambles and eventually gets to the child, who is still howling into the night. He's covered in shit, the stink is unbearable. Gagging and bleeding, Auntie Encarna hugs him close to her chest and starts to call to her friends. Her cries have to travel all the way across the avenue, it seems unlikely that they could possibly hear. But the travesti bitches of Sarmiento Park in the city of Córdoba have much better hearing than your average human. Auntie Encarna's summons reaches them because they can smell the fear in the air. They are suddenly alert, their skin puckered with goose bumps, hair standing on end, lungs taking in as much oxygen as they can, jaws clenched.

"Travestis of the Park! Come! Come look what I've found!"

A three-month-old boy abandoned in the Park.

Covered in branches, left for death to have her way with him. Or maybe the stray dogs and cats that live there: children make for a tasty morsel wherever you come from.

The travestis come over curiously, they look like a pack of hungry zombies stumbling toward a woman with a baby in her arms. One puts her hand, a hand big enough to cover the sun, to her mouth. Another declares that the child is gorgeous, a peach. Another immediately starts to back away, saying that she wants nothing to do with this, she hasn't seen a thing.

"Figures...," says another, meaning that when push comes to shove, you can't trust a hairy faggot.

"We'll have to call the police," says one.

"No!" barks Auntie Encarna. "Not the police! You can't give a child to the police, it's the worst thing you can do!"

"But we can't keep him," says a reasonable-sounding voice.

"The boy stays with me. He's coming home with us."

"But how are you going to get him home? He's all covered in shit and blood."

"In my purse. Look: he fits perfectly."

THE TRAVESTIS walked from the Park to the area by the bus station at a remarkable pace. They were a caravan of cats, hurried by circumstance, their heads down to make themselves invisible. They were going to Auntie Encarna's house. The queerest boardinghouse in the world, during desperate times it had offered shelter, protection, succor, and comfort to an endless stream of travestis. They were going there because they knew it was the safest possible place for them to be, carrying the baby in a purse. One of them, the youngest, worked up the courage to say what they were all thinking.

"It's a cold night to spend in jail."

"What?" Auntie Encarna demanded.

"Nothing, just that prison is pretty cold this time of year. Abducting a baby ..."

I was scared half to death. I trailed behind and kept having to break into a trot to keep up. The sight of the baby had hollowed me inside, as though my organs, blood, bones, and muscles had all been scooped out. It was partly panic and partly determination, two emotions that always go hand in hand. The girls were nervous, their breath billowed in the cold air as they panted in fear, praying to every saint they knew that the boy would stay asleep, that he wouldn't start squealing as he had just a few moments ago, like a pig in the slaughterhouse. Along the way, they were passed by cars driven by drunk drivers, squad cars that slowed down when they saw them, insomniac students out for a pack of cigarettes.

Just by bowing their heads, the travestis pulled down the cloak of invisibility that was given to them when they were baptized. They pretended to be lost in thought, repressing their terror of getting caught. Oh, to truly know fear you need to be a travesti carrying a blood-soaked newborn in a purse. They got to Auntie Encarna's house. A large, pink, two-story building that looked a little run-down but welcomed them with open arms. They walked down a bare passage and went straight into the patio, which was surrounded by glass doors in which the faces of other travestis appeared looking extremely curious. A falsetto voice singing a sad song upstairs was silenced by the commotion. One of the girls got a basket ready, another ran to the pharmacy for diapers and baby formula, another fetched clean sheets and towels, another lit a joint. Auntie Encarna murmured to the child very quietly, a litany, a lullaby, a spell to stop him from crying. She undressed the boy and took off her own shit-stained dress as well. Half-naked and surrounded by friends, she bathed him on the kitchen table.

Some were bold enough to make jokes, even though their asses were clenched like a vise over the insanity of bringing the kid home. Keeping him as a pet, like a rescue dog. They started to wonder what his name was, where he came from, who the terrible mother that abandoned him in the Park might have been. One ventured that if she was planning to throw him in a ditch she wouldn't have named him. Another said that he looked like a Twinkle in Her Eye. Another dismissed this as poetic nonsense, reminding her of the danger they were in. The police were going to come roaring in with their sirens, guns blazing, the news programs were going to shriek bloody murder, editorial pages would fume, society, always up for a lynching, was going to bay for vengeance. Travestis and children don't go together. The very sight of a travesti carrying a baby was a sin to these people. The bastards preferred to hide them from their children, to shield them from the degeneracy of which man is capable. But even though they were well aware of all this, the travestis supported Auntie Encarna in her crazy endeavor. It was the orphans' code.

ONCE THE BABY was clean and wrapped up in a sheet like cannelloni, Auntie Encarna sighed and went off to rest in her room, which was decorated like a sultan's bedchamber. Everything in there was green, hope was in the air; it was the light. Her bedroom was the place where good faith was eternal. Little by little, the house settled down. The travestis withdrew, some to go to bed, others back out onto the street. I collapsed onto a sofa in the living room. The starving child had been given a bottle and they'd grown tired of gazing at him, trying out names, deciding whom he resembled. Once he was done crying, the boy started to look at them with intelligent curiosity, straight into each of their eyes. It was a shock, they'd never been seen like that before. The pink house, the most travesti house in the world (plants in every window, entangled with other plants, fertile plants that sprouted flowers like fruit, in which the bees danced), had suddenly gone quiet so as not to scare the child. Auntie Encarna bared her silicon breast and brought the baby to it. The boy sniffed the giant, hard tit and calmly latched on. He wasn't going to get a drop of milk out of that nipple but the travesti in whose arms he rested pretended to nurse him, singing a lullaby. You've never truly slept unless you've fallen asleep to a lullaby sung by a travesti. Maria, a very young deaf-mute waif, slipped past me like a succubus and opened Encarna's door gently without knocking. She was met with the scene. Auntie Encarna suckling a newborn with a breast full of aircraft oil. Auntie Encarna was a couple of inches away from the bliss into which her whole body was settling, the boy was drawing a lifetime's worth of pain out of her. It's the best-kept secret of wet nurses, the pleasure and pain of being drained by a kid. A painful injection of peace. Auntie Encarna's eyes had rolled up into the back of her head, she was in absolute ecstasy. She was whispering, shedding tears that bounced off her tits and onto the baby's clothes.

Maria brought her fingers together pointing upward, asking Encarna what she thought she was doing. Encarna answered that she didn't know, the boy just started to suck on her tit and she didn't dare pull him away. Maria the Mute made a cross over her breast, pointing out that Encarna couldn't nurse a child, she didn't have any milk.

"Doesn't matter," Auntie Encarna answered. "It's symbolic."

Maria shook her head disapprovingly and closed the door just as gently as she had opened it. In the dark, she stubbed a toe on a table leg and covered her mouth to stop from crying out. Her eyes filled with tears. When she saw me on the sofa, she pointed to Auntie's room and used the same finger to draw circles around her temple: Encarna's gone nuts. It's symbolic. The symbol of a woman obeying the urges of her body, like Romulus, Remus, and Luperca.

FROM THE SOFA I commandeered as my bed that night I remembered what they used to say at home about when I was born. My mother was in labor for two days, she was never able to dilate and couldn't stand the pain. The doctors refused to give her a cesarean until my father threatened the head doctor. He put a gun to his head and informed him that if he didn't operate on his wife to let the child out, he'd be dead before the night was through.

Afterward, people used to say that I had been born on pain of death. My father would repeat this approach, again and again, forever after. Everything that brought me life, every desire, every love, every decision I made, would be subjected to threats. My mother, meanwhile, said that after I was born she had to take bromazepam to get to sleep. Which was probably why she was so unenthusiastic, so passive, about her newborn son. Precisely the opposite to what was going on behind that door, in the room where the light was still on. A green glow to dazzle death, threatening her with life. Warning her to stay back, to forget about the child found in the Park, warning her that she no longer had jurisdiction on the matter. From my sofa, covered in coats belonging to other travestis, I fell asleep to the sound of Encarna's lullaby. The story of my painful birth, told to me a thousand times, dissolved like sugar in tea. In our house of travestis, sweetness leavened death. In that house, death could be beautiful.

IF ANYONE wants to examine our homeland, the homeland for which we have sworn to die countless times in school playgrounds, the homeland that has taken the lives of young men and women with its wars, the homeland that has buried people in concentration camps, if anyone really wants to investigate all that shit, they'd only have to take a look at Auntie Encarna's body. We're like a country too, in the merciless damage done to the bodies of travestis. The marks left on certain bodies, unfairly, capriciously, avoidably, the mark of hatred. Auntie Encarna was 178 years old. Auntie Encarna had scars of all kinds, ones she did to herself in prison (because it was always better to be in the infirmary than in the thick of the violence) and that she got in street fights, from vicious johns and ambushes. She even had a scar on her left cheek that lent her a mysterious, ruined air. Her breasts and thighs were permanently bruised from beatings she'd received under arrest, all the way back to the dictatorship (she said that that was when she had first come face-to-face with the evil of man). No apologies, the bruising was from the aircraft oil with which she'd shaped her body, the Italian mamma's body she used to earn the money for food, electricity, gas, and the water that nourished her beautifully lush patio, a patio that was like an extension of the Park, just as her body was an extension of the war.

Auntie Encarna had arrived in Córdoba very young, when you could still sail a boat down the Suquía River without getting covered in garbage. She had surrounded herself with travestis her whole life. She defended us from the police, gave us advice when our hearts were broken, and tried to emancipate us from the chongo. She wanted us to be free. She told us not to buy into the fairy tale of romantic love. To focus on other stuff, to liberate ourselves from capitalism, family, and social security.

Her maternal instincts were theatrical but took control of her character so thoroughly that they felt authentic. She overreacted like a mother, she was cruel like a mother. She was easily offended and quick to anger. In Formosa Province she'd shacked up with a teamster from Chaco she'd taken a shine to. She was a young woman, she knew poems by Gabriela Mistral by heart and said that her dream was to be a rural schoolteacher, but she earned her living from the trucks. "Being a trucker's whore is something else entirely, another world. Truckers are important men on the road, they're a big deal." Even when she'd settled down in Córdoba, by the Park, having willingly left her past behind forever, she regularly toured the rural towns where teamsters tended to stop for the night. She'd injected aircraft oil into her breasts and butt, hips and cheeks. She said that in addition to being cheaper, it held up better when you got knocked around. But the areas where she'd injected herself turned an unpleasant bruised color and the liquid had run all over the place, lending her body a lunar landscape feel that forced her to work with the lights turned down very low.

She had two nasty scars on her left knee from bullet wounds, the projectile had sailed right through and on rainy days she was usually to be seen limping to the kitchen for a glass of water to take a painkiller.

Rainy days were cause for celebration: we didn't have to go out to work. Or if we were already out and the heavens opened, we'd all pack into cabs and head for her house. Along the way the cab drivers would piss themselves laughing with us, and hearing them laugh we knew that we really were funny, that we were worth something, that we did good too. We played cards, watched porn movies or soap operas, and gave advice to the rookies. After the baby arrived we also turned ourselves into authorities on child rearing. But we kept the secret. Maria the Mute took care of him when his adoptive mother had to go out to do chores. No one could know that we had a baby in the house. We were fully, recklessly committed but also aware of our responsibility. We knew that nowhere else would the baby get so much attention and affection. Simply put: in Auntie Encarna's house he was loved.

We eventually christened him after a democratic vote. A majority chose to call him Twinkle in Her Eye. And it was very fitting because Auntie Encarna, and everyone else to tell the truth, recovered their twinkle whenever we were with him. The moment we got to the pink house, we'd ask: "Where's Twinkle in Her Eye?" and go straight to pick him up, cooing over how handsome he was. We often found ourselves saying things like "When Twinkle in Her Eye grows up," developing a language that was all our own. Or sometimes we'd just ask where Maria was and someone would say: "In there, talking to Twinkle in Her Eye," and we'd go over to watch in heartfelt amazement as Maria's hands flew around when she spoke to the child who stared back at her bewitched, restoring the twinkle in her eyes too.

Twinkle in Her Eye was dark-skinned and chubby with melancholy Asian eyes. As the days passed he grew stronger and stronger, cried less, and began to smile at us. I'd help out with songs and rock him to sleep in my arms. "Say hello to Auntie Camila," Auntie Encarna would say when her arms grew tired, handing him over. I'd take him on a tour of the house. Sometimes I'd sit on the terrace and think about a child, a husband, a house, a patio with flowers in pots, a study, entertaining friends on weekends, giving up prostitution, reconciling with my parents.

RAINY DAYS were also cause for celebration during my childhood in Mina Clavero, the town that bore witness to how I began to turn the body of a son born to a poor young couple into a travesti. When it rained in the summer, I didn't have to go to work. Because I was born into poverty, my lot was to toil. "You need to learn how to earn a living from a young age," my father told me. So I'd sling a cooler full of ice creams and popsicles across my back and go down to the river to sell them. The word was shame. There was no greater embarrassment than having to parade proof of my poverty. Begging people to buy ice cream from me, learning the craft of salesmanship, which I'd subsequently put to use selling my body: I had to tell my customers what they wanted to hear. A shitty little town on a shitty little river.

Which is why rain was always a blessing. When it rained, I didn't have to go down to the promenade to sell popsicles to tourists, who were the worst back then and still are today. Because our household was poor, child labor was seen as a very noble way to pass the time. I worked to pay for my school uniform and supplies while my school friends were on vacation. At nine years old I had to put up with the pity with which the tourists regarded the poor fairy boy selling ice cream. The progressive ones thought I was being exploited, like the kid who invited me into his tent one day to show me his enormous, hard, perfect cock. He asked me if I liked it and I said that I did. He asked me to stroke it but said that I should be careful because it bit, and I put my polystyrene box full of ice cream to one side. He told me to take one out and rub it over his penis and my mouth froze up around it, I got scared and didn't like the taste and it all went to hell because the ice cream melted over his pubis, making it sticky, and he told me that I was good for nothing, a phrase I'd often heard from my father. He threw me out of the tent, warning me not to say a word about what had happened, and I wandered off from the river counting the few bills I'd earned from the ice cream sales. I went home pretending that I felt sick. And, in fact, the moment I said so my temperature rose and I was allowed to stay at home for three days thinking about the dank tent, the guy's scent, his beautiful penis, and its horrible taste. To this day I can't understand what it is we like so much about such an insipidly flavored piece of flesh.

"*COCKS DON'T TASTE* of anything," Auntie Encarna used to say. She'd give you a pat and say: "Bow your head when you want to disappear but keep your chin up the rest of the year, girl." And she was like a mother, like an aunt, to us. Loyalty had a lot to do with why we were all standing around looking at the boy stolen from the Park: Auntie Encarna had taught us how to get by, how to defend ourselves, and how to pretend we were lovable people beaten down by the system, to smile in the supermarket queue, to always say please and thank you, always. And sorry too, very sorry, which is what people like to hear from whores like us.

So, from the moment I met Auntie Encarna, I got used to lying to common folk, saying please and thank you whoever they might be, and sorry too, in all its different incarnations, so people would feel good about themselves and leave you alone for a while.

Every slight lingers like a headache for a few days. A painful migraine that can't be soothed. The insults, the mockery. The heartbreak, the lack of respect. The wheedling of customers, their outright scams, exploitative chongos, submission, idiotically kidding ourselves that we're objects of desire, loneliness, AIDS, broken heels, deaths, murders, internecine feuds over men, gossip, he saids and she saids. It never seemed to end. The beatings, on top of everything else, the beatings the world dealt out to us, in the dark, when you least expected it. The beatings that came immediately after fucking. It'd happened to all of us.

Auntie Encarna said that men's penises were the least important things in the world. That we had our own dangling between our legs and we could always grab them in moments of weakness. She said that we had to work for ourselves, not to pay for whatever the chongo wanted us to spend our money on. And when we slept with a calamity (which is what we called people we slept with for pleasure rather than money), we should make them pay for our bodies in some other way. She also said that after her 178 years on this earth the sorrow had sunk deep. Sometimes she felt as though her legs were like bags of cement, that her organs had petrified and her heart had grown stiff with lack of use. She shed tears over the strictures that kept us down. Like Maria the Mute whom she'd practically brought back to life. When she found her curled up in a dumpster, malnourished and flea-ridden, and taken her home. She had given her a family, the older travestis were her godmothers, the christening was like a neo-realist film.

At the age of thirteen, after a week in the pink house, Maria had been christened as a travesti. The ceremony was held on the patio. While everyone was eating nougat and drinking cider, one of the cactus flowers suddenly opened, right in front of everyone, and started to give off a rotten smell that they found deeply unnerving. One of them wondered aloud how a flower could possibly smell like that, while a know-it-all answered that some flowers are pollinated by flies so give off a bouquet of rotten meat to attract them. But that doesn't make them any less beautiful or alluring, and they have the power to silence a group of travestis in the middle of a ritual of christening and loyalty

This was during our clan's flower period, which flourished in spite of the death sentence that loomed over us. It was a time when we'd sniff each other like dogs and cross-pollinate. The arrival of Twinkle in Her Eye had turned our resentment into a yearning to improve ourselves. Tucu signed up for classes to get her high school diploma: she didn't want to die before she could show it to her mother and say, "Here you go, and I did it all myself, see?" But she was treated so badly at the school where she registered that after her very first day she turned up at the Park bawling her eyes out and started to scream that she was going to fuck around without a condom until she was sick of it. What did it matter, anyway? Auntie Encarna had slapped her silly that night and sent her back to the house to rest. Rest cured all ills. Whether the sickness was one of body or soul, Auntie Encarna always prescribed rest. It was the biggest gift any of us had ever received: letting us sleep while she kept a lookout.

We lived in her orbit. There was always something to eat at her house and we were often hungry. She'd welcome us with open arms and bread on the table. By day I lived the life of a mediocre student. I was poor, I can admit it now, I went hungry. Living off bread alone distorts your body, it makes it sad. Food without color is depressing and demoralizing. But Auntie Encarna's cupboards were always full: if you needed something she'd give it to you. Flour, sugar, oil, maté tea, which was a staple of every home. And she told everyone that another essential was an image of the Virgin of the Valley, who was dark-skinned, rebellious, and powerful enough to change your fate.

WE'D ONLY KNOWN Auntie Encarna to have one real love affair: a quiet, lasting romance with a headless man. Around that time a large number of refugees from African wars arrived in the city. They came to our country with the sand still spilling out of their shoes, saying that they'd lost their heads in combat. Women went crazy over them for their legendary gentle ways, sensuality, and playfulness. They'd endured plenty of hardships during their wars, suffering almost as much as travestis in the street, and that made them both desirable and heroic. The Headless Men took intensive courses in Spanish so they could speak to us, which was how we learned that having lost their heads, they thought with their entire body, only remembering whatever they'd physically touched. The Headless Men arrived with their novel sweetness and gently let down the women waiting for them with open legs and flaming pussies because they much preferred the travestis of the region. We didn't know why they chose us but a lot of us married and grew old with our decapitated lovers. They explained that they fell in love with us because we were easier to share the trauma with. They could let it climb up the walls or suppress it when necessary. But the women were offended by the snub and started saying sly, malicious things about our guests, men who at the end of the day had fought for a better world. They said that making love with them was like going to the beach, afterward you had sand in your ass for days and days. But we didn't care what they said.

Auntie Encarna met him at Hangar 18, the seediest gay club in the city, the most sacrilegious, Dionysian dive around for dykes, faggots, and queers. The relationship between Encarna and her Headless Man had begun as a very lucrative commercial arrangement, at the time Auntie was taking maximum advantage of her body. Customers didn't take anything out of her. She could sleep with ten men a night, not that that happened very often, and wake up the next day fresh and vigorous as a summer breeze, entangled with her Headless Man, who lived comfortably in his own apartment on a veteran's pension. The Headless Men came from regions that were a mystery to us thanks to our lack of education. We never did learn the causes of the bloody conflicts that had driven them to our city but they were everything a travesti could hope for. Of course, there weren't enough to go around: a lot of them ended up in asylums or decided to move to towns by the sea. But the few who stayed in Córdoba soon settled down and the leak was sealed. Their ageless courtship was an oddity in the life of a travesti. He didn't just love Encarna but everything around her, us included, her honorary daughters. Seeing Auntie Encarna in that man's arms allowed us to hope that someday someone might hug us that way. The Headless Man was the life of all our gatherings and sometimes he'd even invite us to dinner at his apartment. We all went, not just to avoid Auntie Encarna's wrath—she could be more vengeful than the saints and Greek gods put together—but because we wanted to experience his understated hospitality for ourselves, see his watercolors, his feisty dog who slept at the foot of the bed, the endless rows of books on his shelves, which we'd never be able to read even if we did have the time because they were written in a foreign language. I was especially fond of him because one night he saved us, Maria the Mute and I, from right out of the clutches of the police, very close to the pink house. One of them had already started to get violent and had me bent over the car because they'd received reports that a pair of travestis were stealing from the local grocery store. The Headless Man came out of the shadows, approached us in his usual affable manner, spoke to the cops for a couple of minutes, and they let us go. The word of a decapitated man counted for more than anything we might say.

According to Encarna, the Headless Man prayed to his gods before the sun came up with the glorious demeanor of a headless mystic, receiving a fresh injection of life from the first rays of the sun. Then he'd go to the kitchen to put the kettle on as he set out the ingredients for the maté the way his tyrannical girlfriend liked it: a pinch of beebrush, a little peperina mint, the maté leaves (with the dust filtered out), a spoonful of honey, and a twist of orange peel. Then he'd go to the bakery and come back with recently baked medialuna croissants so fresh they fell apart on the tablecloth. He'd always get back at the precise moment the kettle came to the boil for the first mate of the day.

Then he'd go to wake up Auntie Encarna, which was more like rousing her from a fairy-tale curse than sleep. She'd roll around in bed and condescend to be adored: "You're look-ing beautiful today, my love," were the first words our adop-tive mother heard every time she woke up there. And it was enough to block out the horror of the world. A brief spell to banish all thought of day-to-day survival, avoiding death, the deaths of our sisters, other people's misfortunes, which were always ours too. At one point they even announced that they were going to get married and chose me to be the maid of honor. They'd be married by our medicine woman La Machi Travesti, the only person with enough gravitas to officiate at such a ceremony, who provided guidance to our body and soul. She was just as capable of knocking us out with her brews of roots, lianas, and cacti as she was of taking us back to the origins of our pain. She also administered injections of liquid silicon, and all for the same price.

But the wedding plans were postponed, more because of her than him. She was always trying to save the world, the little, pink travesti world she'd built to encase her loneli-ness. Auntie Encarna could spend all night sitting in a police station to get one of us out of jail and was just as willing to spend the whole day driving a virus from our body or helping us to remove an ingrown hair on our upper lip. But the love between her and the Headless Man remained strong. He'd visit every Friday afternoon, just when children were com-ing out of school, so we always associated his arrival with the childish giggles and squeals we heard on the sidewalk. He'd stay until Monday morning and then disappear until the following Friday. On the nights he was with us, when Aun-tie Encarna had fallen asleep and had begun to snore like a

Minotaur, he'd sneak out of her bedroom and sit in the patio if the weather was fair, or the kitchen with the burners on if it was cold. He'd set his headless body to contemplation, because the Headless Man was a born insomniac: it's well known that insomnia is a common affliction in his homeland. We saw him as one of our own, so we took advantage of his kind nature and asked him to help with our makeup before we went out. He always remembered our birthdays and was attentive to our aches and pains.

The Headless Man was also a talented guitar player. We delayed our departure for the Park when he started to play sad songs that made us cry women's tears and wonder why the night was so long. Sometimes Auntie Encarna joined in and sang her tragic songs with gusto. At such times the whole world came to a halt. Extremely dark birds perched on the walls and balconies and we all sat still, not daring to blink or breathe for fear that a false move might break the spell. Seeing the two creatures make music together was like watching them make love, an act so elegant it didn't require privacy.

In the kitchen, a plaster image of the Virgin of Guadalupe looked down at us from the refrigerator, and one of the nights on which we stopped to listen to Auntie Encarna sing accompanied by her boyfriend's guitar, the Holy Guadalupana started to cry along with the song, the tears running down her varnish. We never knew if the miracle was caused by the humidity or a divine manifestation, but whatever it was it was a striking image and our hearts almost burst with the beauty of it. He had obviously been moved too, because a couple of days later he brought a notary to the house and had Auntie Encarna read some important-looking papers in which it was stated that if something were to happen to the Headless Man, his belongings would be passed on to her. We watched Auntie Encarna witnessing the will and couldn't help but notice the ambitious gleam in her eyes, or the grimace of disgust at having to use her male name. We knew all about Auntie Encarna's avarice and the will unsettled us a little. When the notary left and it was only us there, Auntie Encarna announced that she was feeling especially generous and sent out for a bottle of champagne, as though she were celebrating. Just then the TV announced that the iconic drag queen Cris Miró had died and we all gulped and fell silent.

I WAS JUST THIRTEEN, I didn't yet understand what was going on inside me, I couldn't put words to any of it. And then Cris Miró appeared on television. She was on all the most popular shows because she was the first travesti showgirl in Argentina, the first to be recognized by the media. Cris on the grandest sofas of the small screen with the blondest, stupidest, most conservative hosts around. And she was prettier than them all. She had hair down to her waist, black and curly, like a wrinkled rug framing the most beautiful face I had ever seen, a face with a dignity, peace, and friendliness inconceivable on the frightful television landscape of the time. And so I learned of the existence of travestis. I was just a child when I first saw her on TV but I immediately knew that I wanted to be like her. That was what I wanted for myself. The uncertainty of transvestism, the disorientation of the office. The epiphany was such that in spite of all the obstacles in my way I too let my hair grow long, chose a woman's name, and from then on kept my ears open to the siren call of my vocation. We all admired her, we all loved her. She was an example. She was the best of us on display for all to see. So news of her death depressed and silenced us. We couldn't stomach Auntie Encarna's champagne: our Evita, our model and guiding light, the most famous and best of us all, had died. No one spoke, no one knew what to say about someone dying so young. But our shared gazes said everything. How absurd that on the same day that Auntie Encarna was named the Headless Man's heir, such sad news was announced to the world. I still remember that silence and what La Boliviana said from the back of the patio: she didn't like Cris at all. She had a very square jaw, she said. We all told her to shut up in unison. To get out of our sight.

WHEN THE BOY CAME to the boardinghouse, things started to change between Auntie Encarna and her Headless Man. We thought that now we had our own Jesus, Mary, and Joseph, our own holy family, a family that reflected us, and we were their daughters. We couldn't think of a better father for the boy than the Headless Man: men like him came from far away, they knew stories, they told you what you wanted to know about the world. They were the occasions one is so grateful for in the monotonous life of a prostitute. The Headless Men who brought suitcases full of recipes for exotic dishes, medicinal plants, new ways of planting in water and the air. New ways to love. Men like him taught us foreign languages, they had moves we'd never experienced before, they made our skin feel thin as crepe paper, as though we'd turned transparent, as though suddenly God could see right inside of us.

But Auntie Encarna started to get brusque. She began to sabotage the Headless Man's visits, allowing the monster inside of her to lash out with poisonous comments about his generosity, freedom, the exaggerated kindness with which he treated us, as though we were all his girlfriends. Who did he think he was? Had he forgotten that he'd been a john, that he'd paid for her?

The first time that the Headless Man tried to pick up Twinkle in Her Eye, Encarna looked him up and down and declared that no child of hers was going to be held by someone without a head. Maria the Mute, who happened to be there, read her lips and scolded her instantly. But Auntie Encarna had located her character, she knew from whence her water flowed and she wasn't ready to turn off the spigot. The Headless Man, friendly to the last, simply backed away to the door and asked what they needed, he had contacts that could help out if she wanted to adopt the child officially and once the wars were over he'd take them both to his home country, Auntie Encarna and Twinkle in Her Eye, to eat the fruit from the baobab tree that fed the Headless Men. It was what made them sweet as honeycombs.

In reply, all he got was insults, attacks, unfounded claims, and mockery of his good nature. But he refused to snap. He

put up with it and put up with it and put up with it. Until one
afternoon Auntie Encarna decided not to open the door and
forbade the women of the family from saying a word to him on
pain of exile, excommunication, banishment—there would
be no exceptions for such a betrayal. The Headless Man stood
for a couple of days under the lamppost on the sidewalk opposite. Then he left without saying a word and we never saw
him again. Some of us, feeling sorry for him, would drop by
his house hoping to find him with his apron on, making the
delicious treats he cooked only for us, but no.

The days passed and things began to settle like mud in
the riverbed. They grew solid and familiar. The thrall in
which Twinkle in Her Eye held us made up for our sadness
over losing our stepfather. And the moment we'd forgotten
him the doorbell rang during a soap opera and we found five
Headless Men standing at the door, elegant and doleful, asking for Auntie Encarna. We went to get her and she came out
with the child in her arms, a little in self-protection and a little to intimidate them. But the Headless Men just handed her
a stiff red envelope containing the letter Auntie Encarna's
boyfriend had written to say goodbye. It said that on no account should she feel guilty, he'd grown a little tired of life,
it was just that, and if she didn't want him any more then he
didn't want to know any more about it. He had been happy, he
remembered her bruised skin as a map on which he learned
to plan future trips. He thanked her for her laughter most
of all and the cool floor of the patio in the shade of the potted jacaranda trees. He'd never experienced anything more
beautiful than the afternoon on which she sang a lullaby to

the boy while he played the guitar, it was good to go with a smile on your face even if he no longer had a mouth or head. Finally, the letter reaffirmed her as the heir to all his worldly goods, all his friends and loves, the woman he loved the most on all the earth, the deeply adored, the unforgettable Auntie Encarna, mother of the freaks. The Headless Men weren't invited in, but they didn't mind. They offered their condolences as well as all their contacts, leaving their telephone numbers. Then they departed in a silent, headless procession down the neighborhood streets. We cried so hard that our dresses got soaking wet, our stepfather, the father we had chosen, who had never hit us or judged us or condemned us to mediocrity, had died, preserving his nobility and loving nature forever. Even in his pain he was elegant and discreet as a shadow. He was surely now in travesti heaven, where he would finally be compensated for his broken heart. Auntie Encarna was the only one not to cry, but she asked Maria the Mute to take the child to her bedroom on the top floor and play him a Gal Costa record. Then she locked herself in her room, undid the front of her blouse to free her heart, knelt down by the bed and finally began to sob and sob. She looked out through the window onto the ivy-covered patio and cried deliberately over her guilt at having turned away her headless boyfriend just days before his death.

Outside, in the patio, with tears still running down our dresses, we filled up a paddling pool and gave ourselves a long, peaceful bath, naked, while the afternoon turned red and was reddened further by our sorrow.

THE NAME of the pregnant girl who accompanied us on our clandestine nightly rounds was Laura. She was the only one of us who had been born with a carnivorous flower between her legs, not like those of us who kept a sleeping beast well tucked away in our panties or a vagina sliced open by the surgeon's scalpel. Laura was already pregnant when I got to the Park. Five months, but she carried it well. In fact, it was a double pregnancy, over which mystery reigned because she'd decided she didn't want to know the sex of the two children she carried inside of her. The first night on which I saw her she wore her hair loose and down to her waist, badly dyed, and you could tell that she'd brushed it to death to get an electric gleam that ruined everything. But that wasn't the best part, the best part was that she'd accessorized her long, dry mane with weeds and leaves from her makeshift workplace: the dark areas of the Park where people could fornicate with anarchic freedom. She just lay back and indulged in juicy exchanges with the thousands of men who came looking for her. Even in her current state, her vagina placed her a rung above us. She came and went to and from the Park by bicycle and liked to get her work done early, never later than three in the morning. "So we're still poor," she'd say as she tucked the evening's earnings between her breasts. She said that the pregnancy had saved her, before she'd led a life that was best left forgotten. She'd been imprisoned for two years for dealing drugs. In prison she'd tattooed her own arm with the words MALDITA VIDA adorned with simple flowers in between each letter. Laura was familiar with every vice and mishap, she'd stabbed her father in the back while he was pummeling her mother's face (then she'd dragged him out to the sidewalk and left him there for someone else to deal with). She was just as young as we were, not older than twenty-three. She didn't know who the father or fathers of the babies she carried inside her were, but the moment she found out she was pregnant she took the test to make sure she wasn't HIV-positive and decided to make some changes in her life. She was going to save up everything she could so that when the children were born she wouldn't have to go back out onto the street. She wasn't just a prostitute, she also carried around food to sell in her bicycle basket. Sometimes it was coffee and medialuna croissants, sometimes empanadas or portions of cold pizza. On hot nights she brought fruit that she kept cool with ice and coarse salt. She'd write us little notes that she'd hide in our handbags without our noticing, and when we were looking the other way, she'd surprise us by grabbing our cocks: "Let's see how little Camilita's getting on," "And what's Encarnita up to today?," "Oh, hello Marita," squeezing your sex just like that, like it was nothing. We'd piss ourselves laughing and be grateful for her coarse kindness. It was always a joy to see her arrive on her bicycle, which sounded like a box full of bells, her enormous belly was like a sign of good fortune and her decision to make real change showed us how one could do without almost everything we'd been told we needed to get along.

When she was sixteen, she'd escaped from a juvenile correctional home leaping from roof to roof like a bewildered demon, and had instinctively become a prostitute. When she was twenty-one she blew off the balls of an ex-boyfriend who was also her pimp and knocked out her mother-in-law. More than once she'd flirted with killing herself, one time getting as far as seeing the light at the end of the tunnel. But there she was, still among us, her hair always strewn with the grass that fell around her bicycle like crickets.

ON THE DAY her children were born we were all waiting in the next room, a light-blue living room, clutching every talisman we could lay our hands on. We watched the finale of a soap opera on a twelve-inch TV, paying more attention to the pace of her contractions. Nadina, who worked as a nurse by day, knew all about births because she'd grown up in the bush and had helped her mother deliver several of her siblings into the world, along with goats, cows, and naughty dogs. We were so nervous, the notion that we might be able to witness a birth drove us crazy. For some of us it was our first opportunity to see a vagina that way, full on, and we were thrilled at the prospect, the way you feel when you're about to do something that will change your life forever. The hours passed, the mother sweated, Auntie Encarna and Twinkle were sleeping on a sofa. The wise women had arrived with everything we could carry: gold, frankincense, and myrrh, but also palo santo to ward off evil thoughts, marijuana so the kids would be fun, liquor to attract the sprites, images of the Difunta Correa so they'd never want for milk, and San Cayetano so they'd always have work, to ensure that their lives would be well lived and never cut short.

The air was thick with our demonstrative faith, like smoke in an underground casino. Some of us sang, others said the usual things to the mother, to push, just a little more effort, while we dried the sweat from her forehead. In the intervals between the labor pains she thanked all of us shepherdesses for being there, for having followed the star. Twinkle in Her Eye watched calmly from his spot, which we found reassuring because we knew that he was psychic. When the head of the first baby was about to appear and Nadina's hands got ready to welcome new life into the world, the thought came to me that they shouldn't be born. I wanted to contradict everything my friends were saying: I didn't want them to come out. What I really wanted was for their mother to keep them inside her forever so they wouldn't have to deal with her for their whole lives. I wanted to tell them that it was dangerous here, that the children of prostitutes were never safe. While the others were putting their all into the birth, I was secretly trying to stop time. But the babies were already slipping down the tunnel of life and culture was inevitably about to claim them. Whatever I might want, culture was stronger. Even though here your parents try to kill you, even though your friends forget you, even though men point and shoot. From the sofa, with Twinkle in her arms, Auntie Encarna was crying. *I gave birth to you too,* she seemed to whisper to her little kid, *but through a path of thorns and blood. I too screamed in pain when I brought you into the world. In the face of death I bartered my memory for your happiness, my health for yours. And the gods heard me and told me that you were mine. I took you in my arms and nursed you with the oily river that wells up from my breast, and the sea came to the city bringing with it fish we'd never seen before singing lullabies salty as tears, and the moon swooped low and I gave thanks to the wind because I felt it on your face, and I thanked the sand because it was the patio in our house and there were the wise women with their tacky gifts, scared, their teeth chattering with fear. You came into this world along a passage of blood and ice, when our breath turned to snow and you, King of Winter, where everything goes to die, brought my flesh back to life because it was completely dead, like a handful of dried herbs. Your birth was just as momentous as this one. And I am just as much your mother, even though I don't have an open wound between my legs.*

Auntie Encarna cried and cried as though she felt guilty for not being that kind of mother, the kind in the room next door. As though it pained her that Laura was giving birth the way people normally gave birth. Or maybe she was jealous because for once we weren't all staring at her, because next door everyone was cheering for new life. And it would be that way forever.

Auntie Encarna believed that travestis were barren, dried up like a forgotten creek. The only fertile one among us, the only one who had had two little chicks secretly whicked into her belly by a person or persons unknown, was Laura. And in that brief moment's thought, Laura became her enemy. But what did we know, we were thrilled with the little girl and boy we saw appear in Nadina's arms, the midwife was crying like a bride at the altar while Laura, sitting in the filled bath in which she'd given birth, exhausted by the pain and effort, said that it was the happiest day of her life because we were all there. The afterbirth, guts and blood, floated at the foot of the bath.

"What a lovely placenta," someone said, and we all burst out laughing, jolting Auntie Encarna from her reverie.

"They're born already?" she asked. Then she came over with the boy in her arms and said to the mother, her eyes drowning in tears, that it was one of each, a perfect little pair. "Now you have someone to play with," she told her son before returning to the sofa and we all went quiet.

Nadina stayed to take care of Laura and her two babies for three months. By day he was a very proper nurse and by night she became a six-foot beauty dazzling passersby in the street. The first few weeks went by easily, Nadina took care of everything while the mother recovered from the labor, the travestis went to work and left the house in silence. By the beginning of the second month a romance between Laura and Nadina was kindled as natural and respectful as any we'd ever seen. Nadina had slipped into the mother's heart through her veins, every time she saw him dressed as a nurse: tall, quiet, a man who could speak three languages but was as silent as an onnagata. She came to live with us as casually as you please. Laura had fallen in love with the nurse, but also her friend from the street, and they just happened to inhabit the same body. Used to men and the desperate passion for cocks, at first Nadina seemed to repress the feelings that were putting lumps in her throat and the pit of her stomach. What was she to do about the certainty that someone else was looking at you the same way you were looking at them, that it's possible for a moment to love someone, that one can be saved, that happiness exists? How would someone like Nadina, who'd only experienced love with violent males, know that the gentle, tender love like the one Laura was offering her could even exist? But the presence of Laura and the babies was more than eloquent and the spontaneous Joseph who had unexpectedly come into their lives dedicated himself to them entirely. It was for the best. Laura never went back to the Park. This was what she had saved up for, so she could stay at home with her children, whom she named Nereo and Margarita. They both took Nadina's surname and she officially recognized them as the father. Nadina didn't go back to the Park either. She took more nursing work, providing palliative care to old people on their deathbeds. At night, the two women lay in bed with the babies between them, watched soap operas, and talked about us, the girls they'd left behind in the Park, telling each other that they should invite us for dinner the following night. All of us who thought we knew Nadina, not to mention everything there was to know about travestis, didn't know what to say about her romance with Laura. We didn't even want to think about how they made love, the very thought of a vagina made us dizzy, sending shivers of disgust running right through us. But they loved one another, every night, we didn't know what the secret was but we knew that that much was true, because their skin and hair were so healthy.

Three months into the relationship, Nadina decided to take her family to her deceased mother's home in Unquillo, about twenty miles out of the city. And there they went, to start again in the Sierras that surround the capital. They set up a store selling cleaning equipment. Every now and again Laura would come by the Park with her backpack full of food, not to sell anymore but to share with us. And although she'd stopped grabbing our crotches, she was more outgoing than ever, as though love had broken down her barriers, because her children were growing up healthy and strong.

Meanwhile, life went on and Twinkle was also growing stronger day by day. We'd put him in the winter sun to infuse him with vigor. Auntie Encarna was kind and friendly to us, and organized a meal of gnocchi every Sunday. She hadn't gone back to the Park to work. We knew that she had amassed a small fortune, fattened even more by what she'd inherited from her dead boyfriend. It was whispered that once a young man who had tried to steal some of her treasure had literally been caught red-handed: Auntie Encarna had cut it off with an ax. She'd taken the mutilated victim to the emergency room herself and later turned herself in to the police to make a statement, saying that she'd done it in self-defense. The police got on with her so well that they took her statement and let her go, but not before asking where she was generally to be found, because scars and bruises and all, Auntie Encarna had a fierce beauty. Not all over, hers was a fractured, unforgettable beauty: the rawest kind. Auntie had a bunch of jewels she'd bought for herself over her long life: some Swarovski crystals, a ring of red gold (the prettiest gold in the world), a pair of emerald earrings, a genuine ruby, and a snake studded with diamonds. Sometimes, to show that she trusted you, she'd take you by the hand, lead you into her green bedroom, and take the chest in which she kept her jewels out from under the bed, saying: "Look, look how the lapis lazuli brings out your eyes. Who knows, maybe when I die you'll inherit it." But then later you'd find out that she'd said the same thing to everyone and you'd understand her a little better.

She was eking out as much love, that awful monster, as she could get. Deep down it was all about a feverish need for love. Asking for love, begging for it in a thousand different ways, with the falsest, most cunning ploys that you can imagine. Anything was fair game. But we stayed with her just the same. When a door closes, a window opens, although you have to be very athletic to come and go by the window. The death of her best-ever boyfriend shrouded Auntie Encarna like a shawl and she began to make everyone's life difficult, like a spoiled little girl. But who among us would dare to say anything? Also, the very fact that the boy existed had softened her and she always knew the right cure for every wound. Twinkle in Her Eye had brought back her memory. She'd sit on the terrace, smoking a joint and looking at old photographs. Because she was so old, her earliest ones were on thick, aged cards with sepia images of her wearing sumptuous dresses fit for a princess. Auntie Encarna had always been royalty.

WHEN I was four, six, ten, I cried in fear. I'd learned to cry in silence. At home, with a father like mine, crying was forbidden. You could bite your tongue, take out your anger chopping fire-wood, get into fights with neighborhood kids, or punch the walls, but never cry. And especially not cry in fear. So I learned to cry in silence, in the bathroom, in my bedroom, or on the way to school. It was a private act only allowed to women. Crying. I reveled in my tears, they made me the protagonist of my own queer melodrama.

How could one not cry when their father al-ways drank too much? What else could you do but learn to cry? I was terrified of how violent he got when he was drunk. And the empty house too. The house without my mother, the possibility that she'd died in the street without my knowing.

My parents had married very young. They had a brief courtship that my mother remem-bered nostalgically because during those first few months he had seemed the most attentive and protective man in the world. He had recently separated and had two young children from his previous marriage. She had been left an orphan by her mother when she was a teenager. She'd never had a father. She was raised by her grand-parents in a house in which she had to get by as best she could at a time when everything was un-fair for women, especially for orphaned women like my mother. My mother's mother had died attempting an abortion and the man who had forced her to abort lived in the house next door until my mother went to live with my father.

Everything at home was shrouded in fear. It wasn't a matter of atmosphere or any specific event in particular: fear was my father. I was never afraid of anything as much as I was of my father: not the police or johns or any of the other cruelties to which I was subjected. To be fair, I think that he was also deathly afraid of me. Perhaps therein lies the original source of the tears of travestis: the mutual fear between father and his travesti daughter. The wound follows us travestis out into the world and we cry.

One day I fainted in the street but I didn't know why. As an adolescent I would suffer from occasional fainting fits. This time I woke up with a stiff arm, confused and aching all over. I'd fallen in dog shit and no one had helped me up: people avoid the body of a travesti in the street without even looking at it. I stood up, smothered in shit, and walked home certain that the worst was over: father was far away, father wasn't in the picture, there was no reason to be afraid. The neglect I had suffered in the street came as a revelation: I was alone, this body was my responsibility. And so I forgot my fear.

AT NIGHT, as a child, I would listen to my parents hit each other. Everything is a reflection: I seek out violence, I provoke it, I dowse myself in it like a baptismal font. I'm a prostitute who walks the street at night when other women my age are in bed. I walk the street stalked by violence but also by desire. I participate in the patterns of violence into which I was born, the traditional ritual of returning to one's parents, reviving the same corpse every night. The nights on which my mother cried waiting for her husband, the nights when the johns don't come, when lovers cheat and chongos beat, the nights when my mother would smoke alone in the dark, staring into the shadows, the nights when we shove into our bodies everything that tightens us up, hardens us, the armor of the shadows, the shadow cast by not knowing our true enemy.

The ignorance that bound my mother to that sick marriage and myself to my sickly marriage to the world, the suffocating ignorance, the downfall of my mother of which I am a continuation, like an animal trapped in a cave. My mother burdened with a child who was beginning to disappoint her, poor mother: the effeminate boy who wouldn't be broken by the belt, by punishments, by the screams and slaps with which they sought to cure the horror. The horror of having a faggot son. And even worse: the faggot had become a travesti. Horror of horrors. I turned myself into the woman I am now out of sheer need. My violent childhood, with a father who needed only the least excuse to throw at me whatever he had in hand, who took off his belt to deal out punishment, who grew angry and lashed out at everything around him: his wife, his son, his stuff, the dog. A ferocious animal, the ghost that haunted me, my nightmare: it was all too awful to want to be a man. I didn't want to be a man in this world.

THE QUEER BOY standing in a corner watching his mother smoke as she reads women's magazines. Such a young woman. A woman who could easily be his sister. The boy has heard his mother cry. The horror of a marriage like that, the result of her need to get away from her own family, the enormous responsibility of a father with a wife like that, a wife who doesn't make decisions, doesn't know how to make decisions, or rather makes one decision alone: to let her husband decide for her. It was impossible to get away from the sound of her crying, not when you're poor: every room is shared.

The woman leafs sadly through magazines containing lives she'll never have, privileges she'll never enjoy. And she cries: because her husband is unfaithful, because he's abusive, because this life is impossible, it isn't what she dreamed of, it doesn't match her fantasy.

In his corner the boy draws. Outside the bush plays its part. It makes you want to cry. The boy has no idea how to console his mother. So he draws. And while he observes her, so he can copy her into his sketchbook, he looks as though he's urging her to go, to run off to live a life as a hippie, which is what she would have wanted. To find a man who doesn't insult her, who doesn't hit her, who enjoys the food she makes, who loves her son. Most of all a man who doesn't drink, who doesn't turn into a monster whenever he has too much wine. A man who doesn't hit your son, who doesn't scorn him, who isn't disgusted and angry and jealous of him. Who won't torture him if he finds him putting on your clothes. A man to

42

talk to at meals, a man who doesn't demand silence while he's watching the news, a man who sleeps next to you? who doesn't collapse drunkenly into ditches. When he's done with the portrait he takes it to his mother. It's beautiful, she says without looking at it, before returning to the article.

AND SO, not really knowing how, I began my journey. I started to watch how my mother put on makeup in the mirror, how she transformed her face from that of a sad woman into the beautiful visage that first saw my father, that first bewitched him. I watched her get dressed, beautify herself, and finish the look with perfume and blusher. And later, at night, I watched her get undressed and put cream on her face and hands.

My father was with his lover, his other family. We dealt with his neglect as best we could. My mother had to put up with being an afterthought in her husband's life. She'd become the other woman, visited occasionally by her lover. But I watched her put on makeup and learned. When I was alone, I repeated the ritual in the mirror, tried on her clothes, I was a little bit my mother too. I painted my face and saw the whore I was to become in my boyish features. I looked at myself in the mirror and desired myself, painted as in my mother's magazines, I wanted myself as no one had ever wanted me. And I went further: I fooled around like a little whore with the neighbor boy. We were the same age and played mommies and daddies. I already knew that my place was to be the mommy. We all wanted to be mommies, it's funny how similar our desires were.

PROSTITUTION comes almost as a fait accompli. They tell you you're going to be a whore your whole life. Your father sitting at the end of the table, greedily wolfing down goat's brain with bread and wine, the father who covers everything he touches in grease, informing you of your fate over and over again:

"You know what a man has to do to be a good man? He must pray every night, form a family, get a job. You're going to find it pretty hard to find a job in that little skirt, your face all made up, your hair long. Take off the skirt. Get that gunk off your face. I should whup it off you. You know what kind of job you, sir, can get looking like that? Sucking cocks, my friend. You know how your mother and I are going to find you one day? Lying in a ditch, with AIDS, syphilis, gonorrhea, who knows what filth your mother and I are going to find on you one day. Think about it, use your head: no one will want you looking like that."

I STARTED going out dancing at nightclubs in the center and in neighboring towns. Two girls and I. I was eighteen. I was still resisting becoming a whore who gets paid for her work, this was easier to deal with. The girls were lovely, pretty and supportive, they were curious about my travesti life. They asked questions and I answered them patiently. We called ourselves the Hembras. We were a nocturnal dance troupe. Only occasionally did we do stripteases. We were young, our bodies were desirable. We knew it and took full advantage. The night was the most damaging part back then. Living for the night ages you, it's depressing. The night is a door to a world where everything is possible. Some things can't happen in daylight. And there I was, at eighteen, earning a living in those nightclubs, scantily clad, with little knowledge of dance but confident in my swing and brave enough to take on any beat you cared to throw at me. I was determined not to become a prostitute and thought I'd manage it, that I wouldn't end up like everyone else. But I also wondered who I thought I was to avoid a fate to which so many others had succumbed. I put up with the insults from the crowd, the disrespectful groping, the terrible pay, all just so as not to turn into a cliché. I wanted to be ridiculously unique, but the truth was that my body had already started to sell itself, it was already on display: an item whose desirability depends on the customer. I thought that I wasn't stained by my onstage shamelessness. But I'd already had sex, with and without my consent, I was already worn in, you might say. I was dry, tough, weather-beaten leather inside the body of an eighteen-year-old child.

AT FIRST I'd put on my woman's clothes at one of my friend's houses. Unbeknownst to her parents, she'd let me

work my magical transformation into myself. And so a shy
bookworm metamorphosed into a plump flower. Things
quickly began to get difficult in town and soon none of my
friends was willing to take the risk of letting me indulge
myself. So I decided that I wouldn't be beholden to anyone.
I learned to sew. I'd use whatever scraps of fabric I came
across: old sheets, cast-off curtains, my mother's, aunts',
grandmothers' old clothes, I found a use for everything.
The clothes I made were rudimentary and poorly stitched
but at least I didn't have to ask respectable girls for theirs.
When I was fifteen, I dressed as a whore. Not dressed, I undressed myself with those recycled clothes. It was my first
taste of independence, of rebellion. The next was finding
somewhere to get changed. A few blocks from my house
there was an abandoned construction site. It hadn't been
touched since we moved to town. In that half-built house
I found a place in which to hide my woman's world, where
I could leave my clothes, shoes, makeup, a flashlight and
candles so I could escape to it whenever I wanted and stop
being Cristian. In winter, it was a little harder, but that
didn't matter. The bare, exposed skeleton, made fleshy by
the frost, ushered in my transformation happily, euphori-
cally. The ritual began at my parents' house, when I'd shave
my legs in the shower. It went on with lies about where I
was going to get permission to go out. I left my home as a
shy little boy with his father's admonishments ringing in
his ear, when I had to be back and how I should behave, and
when no one was looking I slipped into my bare brick palace
and turned myself into Camila. The tights I'd stolen from

my grandmother, the dress I sewed for myself from a curtain that stank of insect repellent, the makeup my fellow students, cousins, and mother didn't want anymore. The perfume I slipped into my pocket when the woman at the pharmacy wasn't looking. The shoes I managed to buy in secret, after spending two years saving up every coin my father gave me to spend at recess. I was a thief, sure. What choice did I have? How else could I make the ritual possible if not through lies, deceit, and robbery? I wouldn't have survived without the petty misdemeanors I committed against those around me and their belongings. Everyone unwittingly helped out the girl who'd head out at night to sway her hips down the street. By day she walked around dressed as a boy, walking like a boy, safe in the costume of a boy who wanted to be invisible. Camila was conceived by petty crimes, committed first against my mother, aunts, and cousins, then against my dance colleagues and then the johns. Especially the johns.

ONE NIGHT, when I was seventeen, I went out dancing. I slipped out the kitchen window. I'd left a bag of clothes at the construction site, ready to change into. I'd also left candles and a little flashlight. And the makeup. It was winter. Winters in that town were tough, the temperature often dropped well below freezing, the frosts fell upon the valley like silent, murderous blankets. Because I was a lying faggot, I could easily escape whenever I wanted. I'd lie awake in the middle of our one-horse town, my eyes staring into the black mirage, waiting for my parents to begin to snore in their exhausted sleep. The tired, worn-out sleep of those who spend their waking hours dedicated to the thankless task of piling one stone onto another, just to have a roof over their head under which to suffer as much as those who have nothing. When the snoring began, I crept out on tiptoe, sneakers in my hands, and climbed through the window into the shocking cold of the street. I got changed in the light of a pair of candles with the flashlight shoved into a gap in the wall. I made myself up as best I could with a hand mirror I'd stolen from my mother. At the time I went dancing in the same club that everyone from school went to. My fellow students rarely acknowledged me, my friends slipped discreetly through the crowd while I got jostled, someone might try to trip me up, another would burn my dress with a cigarette but I kept going, in tune with my own world. I danced in the only place where I knew I wouldn't be hassled: the lounge area. Where my fellow club-goers went to kiss without shame, where everything that really mattered happened, that was where I danced. But not in a corner: I danced from one end to the other, among the unfaithful, the horny, and the desperate, full of life, of yearning, full of the woman who wasn't going to stop for anyone.

The routine of slipping out of the house to change into a woman lasted almost two years, between the ages of fifteen and seventeen. At one point I was refused entry to the club I used to go to: some bitch had said she'd seen me pissing standing up into the sink in the women's bathroom. And of course they believed her. The owner quite rudely told me not to come back unless I was dressed as a boy. So I started to wander the center, to show myself off, so that the whole mob of mountain folk could see me properly dressed, and then I'd walk all the way back to my bedroom.

That night I went out the same way I did every night on my walk around town. I was debuting a new pair of nubuck shoes, a kind of moccasin with high heels that was trendy at the time: I'd sacrificed my teas for a year to buy them. But on my way, the heel of the left shoe broke off and I had to head back with them in my hand, walking the frozen streets in just my tights. I hadn't noticed the patrol van following me. When I slipped down a side street that led to my house, the van pulled up. They asked me where I was going and for my ID. I answered that I was going home, that I didn't have any ID on me and that my shoe had broken.

"We can't let a minor wander the streets at these hours. Let's take you home."

I was rocked by fear, picturing my father at the door as I got out of the police van, in a handmade dress stitched together from curtains that had mysteriously disappeared. I told them that I was fine, I was almost there but thank you, and I opened a gate at random and went inside as though it was mine until I heard them drive off. When they were gone I continued on my way, but when I rounded the corner the van came out of nowhere, corralling my travesti body once more. Inside were two officers and a man dressed in civilian clothes.

"You're Sosa's son."

"Get in, we're taking you to the station."

"Does your daddy know you walk around dressed like that?"

I said no.

"Well, we're going to have to tell him. You can't go around like that, it's against the rules."

I began to cry.

"Stop crying and get in. Stop crying, it's going to be all right," said the one at the wheel. Instead of turning for the station, we headed straight down to the river.

I didn't say a word until the truck came to a stop. They told me that if I was nice to them, they could drop me off close to home without my father ever hearing a word about what had happened that night. I thought about the girls at school, insanely curious about their first time, young women wandering the playground with their secrets, whispering to one another about how wonderful it was to make love with someone you truly adore. Even my male friends talked about the magical pain the girls felt, the sacred pain of the first time. And here I was, in the middle of the night in a police cruiser about to experience the sacred pain of losing my virginity. I made my debut that night, with two uniformed policemen and another who I suspect was a policeman too. I had sex with them out of fear of my father. I preferred to lose my virginity, if that's any kind of loss at all, to facing the ire of my father when he found out that his son went out looking for cock dressed as a woman. In full view of his friends, customers, the children of his friends, his neighbors, his neighbors' children. Not giving a shit about his reputation. It was simple, quick, efficient, and caused no collateral damage. They took turns. In the back seat, where there was enough space. While one was at it, the others stood waiting, smoking cigarettes. When they were done they dropped me at the corner of the street my house was on, just as they'd promised, and let me go with the curt, uncomplicated warning that I was never to speak of the incident to anyone.

THAT WEEK at school I trudged around like a spirit who'd lost its connection to the real world. I could barely walk, partly because of the pain, the torn muscles, and partly from the burden of the secret and guilt, the feeling that I'd irrevocably let myself down. I thought that if I was truly brave I would have gone to the station shoes in hand and waited on a bench for my father to come pick me up. I should have owned what was going on inside of me. Instead, I'd let myself be blackmailed. I was there, I was a part of it. It was my decision and I had a right to make it. I couldn't blame myself for that, but I did, I chose to feel guilty about my pain, the blood that dripped out of my ass every time I went to the bathroom, because I'd been consecutively penetrated by three men.

After that, my body had a different worth. It ceased to be important. It was a cathedral to nothing.

THE VILLADAS, the women in my family, started working from a young age as maids paid by the hour. Some even worked as live-in maids. They were all beautiful, with dark complexions. But my grandparents raised their daughters to be maids, in addition to wives and mothers. It was all they taught them, as well as how to be good people and to never take anything that wasn't theirs. They never encouraged them to study or lead independent lives.

A body is a resource, a tool for work. Some get married, some go to clean other people's houses. They enjoy the freedom, they know that they'll make their money quickly, it's just a matter of hours, you put your body to work and that's it. A humble apron and rubber gloves so you never come into contact with other people's filth.

The sisters set up networks of good employers and recommended one another, covered for each other, helped out when necessary. Then they'd wait for the others to get out from work and take the bus home together. They'd go out dancing as a group and tell each other secrets. None of them finished high school. But they'd been taught to clean other people's toilets, make other people's beds, and cook for other mouths. And never to steal, not to touch what wasn't theirs, and not to give in to temptation. Sometimes they even heard their employers say things like "I love you like a daughter."

Years later, I'd find myself cleaning up after other people too: my fellow boarders. Sadly, I hadn't yet come across Auntie Encarna's; when I moved to Córdoba I found a room in a house on Calle Mendoza, a large house with ceilings so high each room had enough space for a mezzanine. Mine had a window that looked out onto the street, and in lieu of rent

I came to an understanding with the owner. Once a week I cleaned the entire house, room by room, and the sidewalk outside too.

IT HAPPENED one night. I was living in the boarding-house in Córdoba. I had finished my classes at the university, and was walking down a deserted street. A car pulled up next to me and the driver asked me what I was doing. "Going home from university," I answered, but he didn't believe me. Then he cut to the chase and asked me how much I charged. I ventured a number, which he agreed to. It was quick and unremarkable. I can't even remember his face or body. It doesn't merit chronicling. When I went to bed that night I didn't feel a thing, not guilt or pleasure or anger. Nothing. The person who went to sleep that night was half what I am today. The other half was being swallowed up by the fate that had always awaited: to become a whore. That is how one gets into prostitution. The father has done what the world asks of him: he has asked his faggot son in every way possible not to become a travesti, a big whore. To deny herself life, to make a pact with God and live without living, to be someone different, to be his son but not under any circumstances to be what he wants to be: what he wants all the world to see. But the revelation can't be suppressed. How can you hide what has already begun to manifest itself right from the heart of the stone, what was lurking inside the stone for one's whole life, something to be experienced, not just put on display?

An untraceable reality, impossible to know where it began, when one decided to become a prostitute. But the body adapts. It's like a liquid that can mold itself to any shape you set it. Muscles harden or fatten, armor begins to form. Full body armor. Your eyes grow shields. You can't be a prostitute without numbing yourself completely.

One night, everything suddenly seems easy. It's as simple as that. Your body produces money. You set a price and a length of time. Then you spend the money on whatever you want: you squander it as easily as you earned it. You've taken the reins. You're now in charge of your fate. Each and every one of us made the choice to be a prostitute. Age is irrelevant. It doesn't matter that Maria is a deaf-mute, that Auntie Encarna is 178 years old. It doesn't matter if you're a minor, if you're illiterate, if you have a family. The only thing that matters is the shop window. The world is a shop window. We prostitute ourselves to make payments on everything we see in those windows.

Just one night and that's it. One night and the money is in our hands, in our purses. The next day, we pay the rent, tamp down the flirting. One night and we can be like them, the prodigal daughters who go shopping, pay off debts, pound on the doors of stores like beasts of consumerism. We pay in cash. We can't owe anything to anyone. We keep to ourselves, a small pack wandering the margins of the world. We save money and give it to them, the same people who eat us up every night. It's possible that these feasts are the result of our isolation. I learned very early on that we are necessary to desire, the forbidden lust that those who dwell on this earth feel for us. It must be forbidden as an eternal punishment, for disobeying the rules. To punish us they say no one will want us. But life couldn't go on without us there, outside of everything. The economy would collapse, every norm and stricture would be burned up in the savagery of existence if we whores weren't there to offer our bodily love. Without prostitutes, this world would founder in the darkness of the universe.

BEFORE I met the travestis of the Park, my life could be summed up by my childhood experiences and the instinctive transvestism I began when I was still just a girl. Until I met them I was completely lost, I didn't know any other travestis, I didn't know anyone like me. I felt as though I was the only one in the world. And in my daytime world, in the university, the halls of the Faculty of Social Communication, and later the Theater Department at the Art School, that was certainly true. My whole universe was the men and women I met at college and the tricks I turned at night.

My solitary nocturnal outings became frequent. I didn't just need the money, I was curious, dazzled by my fateful vocation. I went out looking for customers. I was young, I knew how to tell stories and to lie. I'd talk to them while we fucked, tell them pornographic stories. I got on top of them, rode them, told them that when I was just a little girl an older man put me on his lap and made me play Amazon and steed. Nothing made them squirm in delight more than fantasizing about abused little girls. They'd explode inside of me, almost a girl myself, not yet even a legal adult. I was a cocksucking geisha. That was the niche I carved out for myself in the savage landscape where I made my living.

Soon I began to experience the minor tragedies that cast a pall over the trade. The petty cruelty of the johns. Haggling here, forged bills there, a punch in the car, brutality in bed. My fellow boarders started to murmur about the door opening at three in the morning and my lingering on the balcony in search of walk-by trade. So I started to tour the red-light districts. El Abasto is nasty. La Cañada is for crones, old women who've been there forever. But the Park was a place full of trees that seemed to have sprung up on their own accord. Scattered around randomly, they sank their roots deep and gave shelter to birds without asking for anybody's help. And then there were the travesti prostitutes who are just as necessary as the trees.

I saw them laughing from afar. Auntie Encarna was cackling the hardest. I snuck a little closer and sat down on a bench nearby. The girls looked over at me, whispering to each other. One of them called out an insult. A moment later, Laura, the pregnant woman with grass in her hair, came over to ask what I was doing there. I pretended to be waiting for someone. She didn't believe me and asked me my name. Then she asked me if I had a pussy, narrowing her eyes, trying to work out which side I played for. When I told her I was a travesti she hugged me and practically dragged me back, right into the middle of the group, to introduce me. The subsequent shower of mockery and slights was their way of welcoming me. No one understands that: no one gets how trust and wariness work among travestis, their intuition. That night, the night of my baptism, when I was welcomed into the group with compassion because they couldn't believe how young I was, Auntie Encarna told a story about one of her many lives: how she'd come from Spain, fleeing from

Franco, but was unlucky enough to be met with Ongania's coup. "One bullet's in here," she said, pointing to her knee. "And the other's here," she said, pointing to her thigh. She carried her bullets around with her.

She asked me my name several times that night. She seemed to forget it immediately, which was only to be expected. No one ever uses our names except other travestis. The rest just use the same term for all of us: faggots. We're third legs, excess bulk, cocksuckers, panties with the stench of eggs, perverts, blunderbusses, boilers, Osvaldo on our good days, Raúl on our worst, diseased, sick, all that and more. Auntie Encarna's difficulty remembering my name was just another example of the general amnesia about proper names suffered by travestis, although she put it down to having been hit on the head one too many times. I said it over and over again, Camila, Camila, and she smiled and said my name was very pretty, very womanly, but I knew what it meant: one who offers sacrifices.

When I told them I was from Mina Clavero, some put their hands to their mouths in shock, others said that they'd been there and remarked how pretty the river and hills were. They asked me what it was like to be a travesti in a small town and I said that it was awful, that it was death, but there was nothing more exciting in the whole world. Being the only one was the exciting part. They asked me about the men and I replied that they were very rough, keeping the details of my sexual exploits to myself. Then Auntie scolded us, saying that only faggots started gossiping about chongos before more important questions like whether I wanted to warm my cockles with a sip of whiskey or perk myself up with a baggie of cocaine.

Her husband had been killed in Spain and on the ship on which she'd stowed away with a leather suitcase that had belonged to her mother-in-law, she decided not to die of sadness, not to throw herself into the ocean, but instead to keep going on and live the best life she could.

"Don't let yourself get hit in the kidneys, take it on your legs, your ass, your arms but never your kidneys," she said to me. She'd been peeing blood for a long time. She wouldn't go to the doctor because she said that doctors were always mean to travestis, they made them feel guilty about their ailments.

I immediately saw that everyone was in awe of her and that when danger struck, she was the one who shielded them from the blows. I tucked myself under her wing, under her gleaming feathers. The many-colored bird who protected us from death.

LITTLE BY LITTLE, I became a part of the pack that ranged furtively around the Park. I was the youngest and most naive of the group. I didn't know anything about anything. But the travestis shared their wisdom the way they were willing to share the contents of their purse with anyone who treated them with respect. The travesti heart: a jungle flower, a flower swollen with venom, red with flesh petals. Auntie Encarna got drunk on liquors of every color and flavor. She missed her homeland, Spain, and the longing drove her into an alcoholic stupor that made her slur her words and talk nonsense. Until Twinkle came into the picture, the only pleasure she ever enjoyed was these states of deep drunkenness during which she talked about her parents, the church bells, and her husband, who had been killed by Franco's men. "I love you like a daughter," she once said to me. And she pulled me close to her the way my mother did when my father got violent. Everyone admires alcoholics, unless they happen to have had an alcoholic father, in which case the memory makes them resentful of the spirits that lurk in wine. Mine debased himself in the glasses of white wine he drank in local dives surrounded by cruel drunks who only ever added to the spite of his already painful existence. Insensible from the wine, he'd wend his way down the streets of the town, in his decrepit car or on the ice cream bike, protected by some kind of guardian angel, the wine gremlin that had taken possession of his body, I suppose. Only once did he end up in a ditch, where he fell asleep with the bicycle lying on top of him. My mother and I had to come out to help him back up, crippled by shame and exhaustion, in full view of townsfolk who lost little time in pointing accusatory fingers. We were marked by the stain of my father's alcoholism, a family in disgrace. But however drunk he was, whatever mess he made of himself, he always woke up before dawn to go to work. Incredibly, his body was always able to deal with the vast amounts of poison he ingested every night before passing out.

My mother and father were ashamed of me. They were ashamed to have a fat, effeminate son who didn't know how to look after himself, who preferred to stay inside watching TV or reading a book to playing football with the other neighborhood boys. When we had visitors, he made sure to bring it up at the dinner table as a kind of punishment. These were the worst moments of my life, when my half brothers came to spend the holidays, or when my cousins came around, because I was always the worst: "See? He knows how to defend himself. He knows how to play football. He has a girlfriend." But I was ashamed of them too. Ashamed of our poverty, of how far removed we were from beauty, of my father's drunken binges in full view of the entire town, of having to work from the age of eight as a street vendor, of my father's need to have a son who was good for something. I didn't belong to that family, I was exiled because of who I was, I wasn't mentioned in the pact my parents had made.

FINALLY the day of Twinkle in Her Eye's baptism arrived. Cakes were baked, hors d'oeuvres prepared, the table filled with snacks of many different colors and flavors, cups overflowed with champagne, clerico, and cider for the wrinklies and soda and juice for the girls. Bunting, travestis decked out in all their finery, chongos on their best behavior because we'd only invited the lesser junkies, the ones who still looked good in photographs.

Maria the Mute had locked herself in her room and refused to come out. Ever since the boy's arrival, Maria had been kept very busy. Auntie Encarna had offered her a wage to take care of him and be available at all times with the added inducement of letting her live in the house rent free. To Maria, that meant getting off the street and staying happily at home until the boy grew up, or the police came to take him away, or Auntie Encarna decided to send him back out into the world.

The offer was tempting but it also meant missing out on the gossip while we waited in the Park, the shared vices, handsome, generous customers, a forum in which to parade our wildest selves. Maria thought it over for several days, doing sums, crossing them out and doing them again. Eventually, she went to Auntie Encarna with a counteroffer. She agreed to be Twinkle in Her Eye's nanny and give up prostitution as her landlady wanted, but she wanted two additional things in exchange: the snake broach and the right to be visited in her room by a little boyfriend who worshipped the ground she walked on, a garbage man she was crazy about.

Auntie Encarna agreed to the deal, gave her the broach, and Maria began to take care of the boy day and night. Maria had a short temper, so Auntie Encarna had to use all her wiles and authority to keep her happy. Nonetheless, we all felt we were lucky to have a woman like that among our number, because she was the only one who was able to keep the house on a vaguely even keel, with her good sense, thrift, and policy of never throwing away anything that could be reused. Also, the boy loved her, this boy who lived among us but hadn't yet been presented to the Travesti Goddesses, who looked down and bestowed their protection upon us from our heaven. Maria talked to him in sign language and Twinkle just stared at her spellbound. When he was with Maria, we could hear his rippling laughter from wherever we were in the house, the sound soared through the air to touch each of us, and it was so happy, so definitively uplifting, that our mood always improved accordingly. The fact was that Maria did good to everyone who came into contact with her. If it's true that well-being can be passed on and propagated, Maria the Mute had the gift of spreading happiness.

Because she was the one who generally ran the household and knew all its tricks, we had some difficulty getting things ready for the party in an efficient and effective manner. Auntie Encarna had driven us round the bend with her orders and demands: "Glasses don't go here, wine doesn't get served there, of course we're going to have drinks at the table, someone make sure to season the hors d'oeuvres, someone answer the door, and someone please pick up that damn phone." If we took even a moment longer than expected she'd start ranting about how travestis had been beaten about the head so much we were all idiots, and where was Maria, she was the only smart one in this whole gaggle of daughters she'd adopted.

I was sent to look for her in her room, which I thought was the nicest in the house, nicer even than Auntie Encarna's, which was like stepping inside an emerald. The curtains in Maria's window perfectly reflected her spirit; lace with tassel tips that forever threatened to fly away, the mirror on the wardrobe she'd covered almost entirely with photographs of Ricky Martin, the stuffed animals on the bed, the picture of her mother in a beige frame of varnished wood, and her underwear strewn all across the room like a roar declaring that she was just as much of a travesti as any of us.

"She was like a baby goat," said Auntie Encarna of the first time she met Maria. When I saw her, I too thought of the goats that had been my pets until my father slaughtered them whenever hunger began to bite. As a deaf-mute, Maria made little squeaking noises like a goat in pain. I couldn't picture her being absent from the carnival baptism to which we'd all brought our humble offerings. Why on earth wasn't she standing downstairs with Auntie Encarna and Twinkle receiving the guests? Instead she'd locked herself in her room and refused to come out. It was no use begging her to come down because the goddamn baptism was about to begin and Auntie Encarna was driving us all crazy. Nothing doing. When I finally got inside, Maria was barely there, a tiny little thing curled up on the bed. She tearfully tried to shoo me away, burbling in her goat language. But when a travesti cries and tells you to go away, it's better to stay, because a travesti's pain, on the few occasions when she lets her real pain show, is like a magical spell: it induces a state of melancholy psychedelia and phosphorescent sorrow. Maria eventually gave in and called me over. She lifted her tear-soaked blouse, damp as the Virgin Mary's cloak when she saw her son die on the cross, and showed me one of her left ribs. It had tiny little gray feathers sprouting from it, like a mottled hen. She was sobbing uncontrollably and all I could think to do was reach out and stroke the feathers, assuming that she'd glued them on. No. To prove that the feathers had grown out of her skin, she pulled one out and held it in front of my face. A drop of blood pearled in the spot where it had come from. I thought that she was going to turn into a saint there and then, that that was her fate. How was it possible that none of us had realized that we had a saint living among us? Maria, the scrawny little deaf-mute prostitute who spoke in chirps, beautiful Maria who drooled and asked us to shave her because she always cut herself, was the saint of our church.

The problem was that Maria didn't see it like that. She was terrified. On the whiteboard she used to communicate with us, she wrote: WHOZ GONA WANT ME LIK THIS? What could I say? A man who didn't want a woman who appeared to be turning into a bird was an idiot, eminently forgettable. She erased the board and wrote: HOWM I SPOZED TO WORK? I told her that I'd work for the both of us, even though I didn't mean it. Not even close. She shook her head and buried her face in pillows lined with polka-dot lace. IMA MONZTER, she wrote, barely looking at the board. I took it from her and stayed by her side, stroking her hair and telling her that she was only making things worse because Auntie Encarna would eventually come up to see what the hell was going on and then she'd be exposed in front of the entire hysterical matriarchy.

But Maria the Mute couldn't stand the idea that she was turning into a bird, and I, stupid as I was, couldn't think how to calm her down. I just kept saying, slowly so she could read my lips, that she was only turning into a bird, that I'd take her to a doctor, it couldn't be anything serious. I'd had plenty of experience dealing with all manner of medical conditions in myself and others so I told her not to worry, the feathers were pretty, they didn't even show under her blouse, why didn't we go down to the patio, everyone was waiting for us to do the baptism, the baby was looking gorgeous, like freshly baked bread, everyone there was very nice, nothing could go wrong. Eventually Maria hugged me and we went out into the world. Both of us were twenty-one at the time.

WHEN WE JOINED the party, we found that the baby had been placed in the middle of the patio in his basket of supple branches. Next to him was Auntie Encarna bawling like a mourner at a freshly dug grave and on the other side was the priestess overseeing the baptism. She was dressed in an animal print that made her look like a leopard, stalking the boy with her red extensions tied into a bow over her head and giant nails brushing the side of the basket. This baptism meant something. It wasn't every day that La Machi baptized a boy. Nadina and Laura had tried to get her to do it for their children but La Machi had told them that they weren't ready to be presented to the Goddesses.

La Machi was a hulking Paraguayan travesti who'd once torn off half a policeman's cock when he tried to rape her. Before the ceremony began she drank a dark-blue liquid that looked like ink from a very delicate etched crystal glass. She raised it up with the tips of her fingers and sang a song in Quechua that invoked the earth to welcome the boy with a smile. And so he was inducted into our travesti fellowship, assured that he would be strong and happy and the wind that blew in his face would make him prettier and death would take him gently in his sleep because he would have known love.

Twinkle in Her Eye, baptized in spring, was the travestis' favorite, the boy who got the most gifts from the Three Wise Women, for whom even the simplest, cheapest trinket had a sacred aura. The boy found in a ditch, a child who belonged to all us daughters of nobody, orphans like him, apprenticed to nothing, priestesses of pleasure, forgotten, fallen women. Baptized by a Paraguayan whore dressed as a predator who blew blessings over his face, who scooped up some of our tears with her fake nails and used them to bless the boy's forehead. Twinkle never once cried. In fact, he smiled and midway through the ritual let out a cheeky fart that had us all in fits of laughter. Then came the toast and the usual chatter and Maria appeared to forget about her avian fate. At times like that one wants to be able to remember. At times like that, one gives oneself over to memory.

NEWS OF THE BABY found by Auntie Encarna spread across the sisterhood, and they came from all over to meet him. Dark women from the north, round and sweet as corn, who sang high-pitched rhymes in the evening, the foreigners who said they were just visiting but wouldn't have forgiven themselves if they left without seeing Auntie Encarna's son and having their photo taken with him, like real aunts. The prodigal daughters who had once stormed off with their feelings hurt, or whom Auntie Encarna had cast out of the family for some imagined slight. We all heard the call of Twinkle in Her Eye and wanted to celebrate his clandestine adoption even though we had little more to offer him than our affection. We all swore, on Auntie Encarna's palm, that we'd never tell anyone about Twinkle in Her Eye. We didn't seal the pact with blood because the bug was going around and we were terrified of dying that way. But it was the same as if we had because we were all daughters of the same mother, we'd been born to the same beast and drunk the same milk: that of our mother who gave birth to bitches and prostitutes, to pigs.

Barren, bitter, parched, bad, ruined, lonely, sly, witchy, infertile bodies of the earth.

TWINKLE IN HER EYE had been baptized. If he died he would go to travesti heaven. Auntie Encarna was bewitched. The way she picked up after the party, coming and going with trays, separating the leftovers, washing the glasses, sweeping the floor, taking down the Chinese lanterns that lit up the heresy. We had no choice but to love our mother. Nothing was as beautiful as her. How could we deny our love for her, or for our blood mothers, the monsters who had driven us crazy. The woman standing there, who bore the hatred of the world on her shoulders, was far worthier of our love even if she could be a bitch and a despot, a desperate, lonely woman capable of anything. The woman who fed us when the rest of the world chased us away. Now she had a legitimate son, his adoption was a historical fact. She had had him baptized and she was cleaning up after the christening party.

Like a last emperor in the final years of his life, that was how Twinkle in Her Eye would live in the pink boarding-house, its patios taken over by geraniums and China rose, far from the violence of the city. If violence existed in the house, we had brought it with us in our bodies. We were con-taminated with it. And so Auntie Encarna asked us to take off our shoes when we came in, to leave them by the door, in the wicker rack. Our shoes sat together in exile while from inside, barefoot and curious, we laughed at them. Some of those shoes were enormous, horrible, size thirteen or four-teen, some looked like ocean liners crammed into Auntie Encarna's dock.

The truth is that for a while, before the fall, the violence of the street never did set foot in the house: it was kept at bay in the soles of our shoes, to protect the boy, to save him. You can't blame us, we had a right to our naïveté.

I WAS STILL A CHILD, I couldn't survive on my own. At night I prayed. I had been taught to pray and I had faith because I was still very young. I had been given a god who fit into a rosary.

One day at a family gathering my father said: "If I ever had a son who was a faggot or a drug addict, I'd kill him. What's the point of a son like that?" He looked around the table. Everyone agreed, nodding their heads, saying sure, what's the point of a son like that. My mother agreed. And because I understood everything related to the femininity wrapping itself around me, I also saw the implied threat. A few nights before, I'd asked my mother why my voice sounded like a girl's, and she said she didn't know.

After hearing him say that he wanted to kill me, I was very afraid. He'd already pointed a gun right at my head. I'd seen him hit my mother, and I'd seen my mother submit to everything he did like a worthless animal. And so I prayed. I prayed for the nightmare, the nightmare of my life, to come to an end. The death wish began when I was very young, an early apparition of the suicide that has haunted me from an early age. I knew that the specter was there, I could see it clearly among other potential wishes, before finding out that becoming a travesti would free me of it, that contrary to predictions, salvation would come in the shape of a pair of high heels and used pink lipstick.

I would spend many nights praying and praying, praying for life to be different when I woke up. At first I prayed to change, to be like what they wanted. But as my faith grew I started to pray that I would wake up the next day as the woman I wanted to be. The woman I felt inside of me so candidly that I ended up spending my hours of prayer praying for her. When I fell in love with one of my little classmates, I prayed to be seen as a girl. When I started to bloom, I prayed for breasts to grow overnight, for my parents to forgive me, for a vagina to appear between my legs. But no. I had a knife between my legs.

WE ARRIVED at midday in a run-down purple truck in which we carried all the shitty furniture my parents had managed to cobble together in their six years together. Just a few chairs and tables, old beds, an enormous wardrobe that was the most valuable piece in the house, a few rickety cupboards and a glass salad bowl my mother inherited from her grandmother. There were also some coffee cups she collected that were lovely, proof of her good taste.

The house we were moving to was by the side of the road from San Marcos Sierras to Cruz del Eje. The village was little more than a collection of houses scattered on either side of the road, forever vulnerable to being overrun by the bush. An abandoned railway split it in two. Even the occasional pleasure of seeing a train pass by was denied to us. I didn't know why I had to leave behind my school friends and my forbidden lover, along with the reassurance of being near my grandparents. Nobody asked me and when I asked I was told not to make a fuss. We lived here now.

To get to the house, we had to turn off the road onto a dirt track and walk up a stone staircase that led to an adobe gallery. The house had a wooden tile floor. My father said that it was very valuable. He managed to buy it as a desperate last resort before his lover and business partner screwed him over definitively, leaving him with nothing but the clothes on his back. The house had an enormous living room at the back that my father had rented out to a whole family: grandparents, a couple, and two children, one of whom was deaf. They were still there. The contract ended when we arrived, but they didn't go, so we were going to have to live with them for a while. The house didn't have an indoor bathroom: there was a latrine in the garden.

Before, we lived in my grandmother's garage. I can't remember why my father wasn't with my mother and me but one day he turned up and a few days later we were loading up everything for the move. We left the town and my Indian grandmother behind to live in the bush. Ridiculous. At least when we lived in my grandma's garage we could use her bathroom, we were nearby and I had grown fond of my aunt Rosa, who was actually a great-aunt but much younger than my mother. Now, at night, if you didn't want to go outside you had to pee in a bucket.

And we had every reason to be reluctant to venture outside at night. The bush was all around us and our neighbors soon warned us of the dangers that lurked out there. Foxes, cougars, snakes, spiders, a whole array of fauna ready to devour us the moment our backs were turned. To compensate for the house I hated, there was a stream that ran next to the garden. It was perfect, you could drink the water, the stream was what fed the well from which we drew water for everything: to drink and wash ourselves and our clothes. The miracle of water.

Because we'd moved in summer, at the beginning of the year, the stream was a refuge during those first few weeks. I spent hours in the water, digging down into the sand to get deeper. Meanwhile, my parents got the old house back on its feet, with its high ceilings and wooden beams that provided homes for bats. My room had a window with bars and high shutters I was never able to open on my own. If I wanted light, I had to ask for it. But, because I was invisible, my room stayed dark all day.

The invisible, displaced kid. Child of the bush. A queer hick.

My father said that when he visited the house for the first time he was told that it had belonged to the family of Doña Paula Albarracín, mother of Sarmiento, the father of education in Argentina. There was a plaque that proved it but I didn't yet know how to read. I'll never know if it was true or not. But I lived in a house with an aura of history.

Meanwhile, the tenants finally moved out and we were on our own. We'd only been in the village for a few weeks. I was going to school, a rural school in which all seven grades were taught in the same classroom, with the blackboard divided into seven sections and the same teacher for all of us. Little by little we got used to this new way of life. There were two stores in the village, one of which charged exorbitant prices that upset and demoralized my mother. The priest came to town once a month to say mass and the doctor visited similarly, seeing his patients in a side room attached to the general store.

Doña Carmen and Don Lalo lived in the house opposite with their teenage daughter. They really were very nice. Sometimes they let me come over to watch cartoons. Our terribly distinguished house didn't have electricity. Just when we'd started to get used to our rustic lives, to counting the cars that passed by on the road to distract ourselves from the boredom, to peeing in buckets so as not to go outside, when I got used to the cruelty of my new classmates, who called me Faggot instead of my name, my father announced that he was leaving. Claiming that he needed to work, he left my mother and me alone in Los Sauces, the asshole of the world. My mother said: "No, you're leaving to be with her." He hit her for her defiance and the next day he left, hitchhiking along the road.

For several days my mother cried and cried and smoked and smoked. If I wanted to know where she was in the big, dark, dangerous house with no electricity, where bats cooed their lullabies, I just had to follow the trail of cigarette smoke.

I became a sad little fairy.

Fortunately, the neighbors took her on like a daughter and everything got easier. My mother, who was twenty-seven, made friends with their teenage daughter and wasn't so lonely any more. But I, stained with the mark of gayness, couldn't make a single friend. I was doomed to the melancholy loneliness of the countryside. The torment of the crickets, the red skies and nighttime beasts. Fortunately the stream was there and the cleansing water washed everything away. On its shores lived a family of coypu. They were like giant, elongated rats with lovely dark gray fur and rarely left the water. And there was also the most handsome boy in school, who was in the seventh grade and sat me on his lap during recess. I loved it when he called me Faggot. Sometimes he took me to the bathroom and made me shove my hand in his shorts to touch his hot, stinky, but tame little snake, which soon got very hard. He taught me how to give him a hand job. We were both lucky, we were never caught. Even at the age of six I knew the consequences that kind of pawing around might have.

The faggot boy attracted to flesh.

SOMETIMES my father brought back animals to take care of. First it was hens. Pretty soon after we'd put them into the garden, built a coop, and learned to take care of them, we woke up one morning to find them all dead. The neighbors reminded us that the bush was full of foxes and big cats, that we had to set traps or the animals would be killed by predators.

My father set traps all around the house. Sometimes, we'd come across a fox dying in pain and rage. Other times it was a cougar. He gave them all the coup de grâce so they wouldn't suffer. But one day we found a coypu, caught by mistake. I was terrified by the hatred I saw in its face. It was no longer the little animal that moved so gracefully through the water, it was a beast out for revenge. The hatred of animals when they fall into traps is made especially clear by the way their hair stands on end. If ever they got free they wouldn't think twice about eating a whole family. They'd gobble up my mother and father and then me.

The anger of the trapped animals was the same that I saw in the eyes of pigs, goats, and other animals that my father slaughtered to sell the meat. My father forced my mother and me to take part in these killings, making us his accomplices in the slaughter. My mother knew to look away while he screamed about how useless she was, to grab the legs harder, to make herself good for something. When it wasn't her, it was me, the useless faggot boy crying in impotence.

Life there was so hard that I thought that something really bad would happen to my father, that one day he'd be eaten by one of the animals, that he'd be gutted just as they were, underneath a pile of hair, feathers, scales, and bloody entrails, because of all the harm he'd done, all the hatred that radiated out from the poor dying creatures trying so very, very hard to escape, sometimes from my mother's clutches, sometimes from mine, giving me unbearable nightmares with their screeching and despair, their agonizing, unending lament. To live in the bush was to live in heat and fury. The father taught the art of cruelty, the mother the art of manipulation. The son learned how to kill chickens at the age of six.

FOR MANY YEARS my fear of the gazes of those ferocious trapped animals stayed with me. They knew they were going to die and from within themselves they received orders to do something, their whole lives depended on fangs that roiled with foam and rage.

It was exactly how my father looked when he drank. He'd been associated with death for so long that the same anger and hatred had embedded themselves inside him. He looked at us the same way the animals did, caught in his own trap. The trap of having been born into the family he was born into.

I only ever saw that ferocity again years later in a fight between two travestis, on one of the many nights when the savage life of the bush appeared to have tracked me down once more. Sometimes you're a victim, sometimes you victimize. On this occasion we were all standing at the doorway of a gay disco, about to have a coffee at one of the little stands they set up in the street. It wasn't yet dawn. From out of the darkness came a body propelled by a stronger force, a travesti falling to the asphalt, contorting herself in her efforts to get back up and sink her teeth into her opponent. It looked like they were going to eat each other alive. They threw a whirlwind of punches that made them look as though they had more arms than Shiva. Shoes, purses, earrings, blood, nails, extensions, false eyelashes, and teeth flew through the air, they snorted shrilly like the pigs when my father hit them square in the forehead with the back of the ax to knock them out.

Those of us who tried to intervene got kicked and scratched for our trouble. When the police tried, they were forced back in the same way. You just had to wait until the fight had played itself out, who knows why it had started or by whom. It's horrifying to see a pair of travestis turn on each other like that. The two of them scrapping with so much blood on their hands they looked like they were wearing gloves, dragged away from each other by other travestis who got our own knocks in the process. We all ended up scratched, beaten, spattered with the blood of one or both of them, paying the price for their ferocity. And we all had to go to the station, forced to make a statement, manhandled in the cars, shoved into cells, wanted and scorned by the police like bearded jewels. The ferocity in their eyes, the hatred in the gazes of the two travestis as they fought: when my father drank too much his eyes looked the same way. All animals caught in the jaws of a steel trap have that look.

ANOTHER LOOK has stayed with me. These eyes screamed too, but this time with tenderness. He came at the beginning of every month, just after he got his paycheck. He moved around on crutches, he was completely lopsided, his legs weak and deformed, but his chest perfect, his face perfect, his hands strong, his arms, toned from the effort of supporting his body, were the most beautiful arms in the world. He brought with him his resentment over his disability, which was only accentuated by the beauty of the rest of him, as though he couldn't believe that that face and body could have come with such useless legs.

He was rough, he'd been desensitized by his condition, but he was breathtakingly handsome. He only paid to sniff between my buttocks, but he did it so voraciously that it felt like he was making love. He spent all his money on a whore like me, the monthly wage he got as a proctor at a secondary school went between my butt cheeks, the opportunity to feel himself coupling with me, our shared pain over wanting to die because of who we were. He'd stay down there until his breath had turned to steam as he worked out his rage, grabbing my thighs hard. I sensed that if I'd have asked him, he'd have made me his wife. I couldn't think of a more achievable paradise than nights with him and his enormous penis to defend me from the world. A man like that, who came with his wages in hand, ready to hand it all over, as sweet and bitter as a tropical fruit.

Then one day I told him that I didn't want to charge him anymore, he could come when he liked but he didn't need to pay me. He was offended. He told me that he didn't want my pity and left, never to come back again. Sometime later, I saw him in the street: he was very well dressed, accompanied by his parents, two small parents, we both had parents like that, but it was his sweetness that was infused everywhere in the street, in the buildings, the hazy trees. I'd recognize it anywhere; his sweetness changes the air, turns oxygen into a vector of affection. He was in a wheelchair. We looked at one another, pretending we'd never met. I repeat here and now that I wanted him for a husband. But everything is different now. Neither his eyes nor mine dare to remember the hot siesta habit, the steam of his breath between my buttocks, the hatred whispered into them like a hole in a tree trunk.

EVERY MONTH, Natali locked herself in a room at the back of the house, guarded by Auntie Encarna with the boy in one hand and a shotgun in the other. The door was locked with a thick chain and an enormous padlock. Natali was a seventh male daughter of her family, so on nights when there was a full moon she turned into a she-wolf. If we didn't watch out for her, she'd end up hurting herself, causing scenes that would subsequently be dismissed as drunken hallucinations by all but the most sensational news outlets, before waking up under the trees with her clothes torn to shreds. Natali's status as the seventh male daughter also meant that by tradition she became the godchild of President Alfonsín, who had been present at her baptism, and since then her whole family and the people close to them had supported the Radical party over the Peronists, even though none of them had shown the least interest in politics previously. Natali cried blue tears every time she heard the eponymous song by Julio Iglesias and claimed to be capable of doing terrible things on the night of the full moon if she didn't lock herself away in the room. And so she had moved in with Auntie Encarna, and asked her to do her the favor every month of chaining her up, drugging her, or knocking her out with a blow to the forehead if she got feisty, because turning into a beast had horrible consequences for her body. Before going out to work, we'd stand by the door for a while to keep her company, singing to her or asking if she felt okay, but she mostly only answered with growls. Only very rarely did she use her whiskey-hoarse travesti voice to say that she would never be completely fine and we should leave her alone.

But there was never any peace for Natali, whose drastic personality changes echoed those of all us travestis, sharing her animalistic curse with Maria the Mute. Poor Natali died young, ravaged by her condition, after aging at an accelerated rate, the way dogs, wolves, and travestis do: seven years for every human one.

The saddest part was that the rest of the time, Natali was very good with Twinkle in Her Eye, she blew on his belly and played peekaboo with him. Natali was so kind that we couldn't square the beast that bared its teeth and growled from the dark room with the little woman with mixed-race features who was everyone at the house's favorite for the rest of the month. But we all knew: Natali had teeth that could grind up human bones like ripe fruit.

We eventually organized the house's routine around her cycle. We said that it was like our pack was menstruating. We followed the lunar calendar knowing that we couldn't let our guard down because we couldn't fail Natali. Every month, we saw her die as she returned to her lupine form, every month she came out a little more run down. There was nothing we could do for her, but she was the bravest of all the travestis I knew, she was a wolf twice over, a beast squared.

During Natali's final few months, we were visited in the Park by a pair of sister travestis from one of the more privileged areas of the city who only became travestis at night: during the day they wore their male masks. They were posh, rich kids. Wherever we went, they would follow us with all the impunity of their class, trotting elegantly along in a false show of shyness, like penitents, until they'd joined the coven of travestis, who greeted them mistrustfully. But then they'd open their Chanel bags and take out the fancy bottles they'd stolen from their parents while they were off traveling the world. To us they tasted bitter and strong, which is what happens when certain people squander their money on luxuries. We didn't know how to appreciate good liquor, it threw us off balance. We were used to the blunt shock of cheap whiskey, gin, rum, or anis mixed with clonazepam or cocaine, or soda if that was all there was. These women with their expensive booze, glowing skin, and imported makeup threw our coarseness into stark relief. Their wigs of real hair, which they'd inherited from their aunts, were quite different from our dry, mongrel mops. We called them the Crows because they liked to scavenge alongside us but we knew that we'd never really know why they came: what could possibly be the attraction of a motley, troubled pack like ours, made up of street girls, runaways? We could only stand it by numbing ourselves into oblivion. But they wore their mothers' lovely blouses, were swaddled in a halo of enchanting perfume, and had come to remind us of our poverty, our lowly origins: our plastic tablecloths, our flimsy, yellow pine furniture, the filthy blankets that had covered the bodies of our relatives before they came to us. And we mistrusted them even more for their male double lives. I won't lie, plenty of us occasionally went back to being male for a while, heading down the path of shame, slipping into our male bodies, the appearance we denied and sometimes even hated. But the Crows brought with them a sickening manly aura that turned our stomachs. It wasn't just the fact that they hadn't come out of the closet, it was that it was easier for them that way. Their ease highlighted our discomfort: we'd never had the chance to hide in the closet in the first place. We were born out of the closet, beholden to our appearance. Which is why, deep down, we hated them. And why they hated us: because they needed us, we were absolutely necessary to them because we reminded them of their privileges. Even though they arrived bearing gifts, even though they condescended to give us the perfumes their mothers didn't think sufficiently fine, or well-used designer clothes or beaten-up purses with glamorous pasts. These leftovers emphasized the chasm between us, much as they protested they wanted to be like us. They copied us but they couldn't get past the class barrier. They spoke our language because of course they spoke several, they imitated the way we walked and fucked our johns but they didn't charge: they did it to indulge themselves, not because selling their flesh was their only option. They were just playing at living someone else's life.

And of course, their reflected glamour turned more than a few heads, giving rise to heightened wants and aspirations. Maria the Mute wanted to dress like them. One day she went to a fashionable store in the center: the salesgirls looked like they'd seen a ghost. Skinny and dark, her arms covered in rows of feathers, mouthing her little chirps. Please, don't get me wrong, it was a nightmare for those posh little shopgirls. Poor Maria was just trying to gain entrance to a different world the way the Crows strode into ours whenever they so chose. But one wasn't allowed to make the journey in reverse: the salesgirls laughed with fear and hostility, called the security guard, and shoved Maria back out onto the street. Until she had fully transformed into a bird, she never again tried to shit above her station.

Auntie Encarna, who had an animal wisdom, was much colder to the Crows than we were. Little by little, she taught us who these two strangers whispering behind our backs really were, these women with a ready answer for everything, who, if they came across us in the street one day would suddenly need to look for something in their backpacks so as not to have to meet our eye, who drove to the Park in the car their daddy had given them but parked it a prudent distance away, who declared that we travestis had no sense of the future, who condemned our lack of taste with a glance. The two strangers, as Auntie Encarna quite rightly called them, had something dead in their gaze: something that told us they didn't know how to lose, that nobody had made it a part of their upbringing. They were only interested in winning, in taking advantage of the opportunities on offer. They were with us because it was the only way they could think to be women without taking any risks.

But still they gave themselves away. With Twinkle in Her Eye, for example. They said hurtful things about him with a naivety that wasn't a part of their character. I didn't buy into it when they bounced him in their arms and neither did Maria.

After the incident in the store, Maria hated them maybe even more than Auntie Encarna. At Natali's last birthday party, she poured a bucket of punch over their horrible, expensive dresses which made them look like a pair of oligarch spinsters who had stayed together so as not to die alone. They made such a fuss, calling her an Indian piece of shit. Then Natali took the butcher's knife she was using to cut the cake, stabbed it into the table, and hissed at them to say it again, daring them to insult her friend a second time. Sly as they were, they apologized immediately with their aristocratic manners, saying that we were all Indians, no offense meant, we're all friends here.

I thought it was dangerous to introduce them to Twinkle. But Auntie Encarna had all the means and contacts to make life difficult for them if they tried anything. One day, only half joking, she told them that if they ever betrayed her adopted son, she knew where they lived and was perfectly willing not just to burn it down but to let all the city of Córdoba know that they dressed up as women and hung out with us in the Park. She said it looking them straight in the eye with a smile, something that Auntie Encarna did regularly with them. "After all, what harm is there in burning down the mansions of families like yours? The founding families, noble families who let the dregs of their wealth trickle down onto the heads of the not so noble. What would the damage be? What is there to lose?" she asked rhetorically, her eyes boring into the Crows. We laughed but we were also unsettled because we knew the threat was more than genuine. And we weren't sure that these bougie women did. As glamorous as they were, they weren't the brightest.

———

DEOLINDA CORREA, the popular saint, worker of miracles, Indian myth stolen by Christians, known as the Difunta Correa, is ten years old. She's orphaned by her mother. She's alone at home in the middle of the countryside. She lies down to sleep. Life is huge and distant.

HER FATHER comes home, drunk. He goes into the room, sees her sleeping, and confuses her with her mother. He bends over her and sniffs the girl's sweat, it makes him dizzy and a little sick, but he still kisses her on the mouth. Deolinda wakes up and is frozen in place by the immanence of life and the night. And so she learns her first great secret.

SOMETHING BEGAN in the dark. I'm talking about my dark now, I'm talking about myself. I'm talking about the feeling of being force-fed fistfuls of dirt by God himself.

ONE NIGHT we found one of our number dead, wrapped in a trash bag, lying in the same ditch where we'd found Twinkle in Her Eye. We found her while hiding from the police, who were touring the area recruiting whores for their jails, looking for outlets for their cruelty. We ran, crossing Dante Avenue like hares on our platforms and stilettos, leaping over the bushes and potholes in our path, diving into the ditch and lying still as dead bodies, which was when the foul smell and the flies reached us. Auntie Encarna ripped open the bag with her nails and met the disfigured face of her friend, which already housed a population of maggots eating her from the inside out. Encarna screamed loud enough for the cry to reach heaven: Why? Why? She took the head of the dead woman in her hands and pressed it against her chest. Tears rolled down her cheeks, all our cheeks. Why? Why? She smashed the head of the corpse on the ground, like she was trying to crack it open. Why? Why? Maggots popped out and flies buzzed around. Auntie Encarna continued to beat the head against the ground asking over and over again through the snot and tears: "Why didn't you defend yourself? Why didn't you defend yourself?" Maria tried to calm her down but Auntie Encarna bit her ferociously and swore vengeance on whoever committed the cowardly act. Killing one of us. Killing a travesti. A manifest atrocity.

MEANWHILE, the boy grew, fed, and slept in Auntie Encarna's arms. He was dark-skinned and vigorous. His needs wailed through the house, driving us crazy. Auntie Encarna had grown round and soft, living off the rent. Finally, at the age of 178 she was able to live a quiet life. The bitter smell of the baby perfumed her bed. She loved him. We all loved him.

The child smiled at us and slept. He was the apple of our eyes. Auntie Encarna, a devout follower of the Difunta Correa, said that the baby was actually the child of the saint. People don't know that part of the story: the baby was raised by a group of travestis working in Sarmiento Park.

SANDRA WAS THE SADDEST travesti in the pack. We were always having to console her over some nonsense or other. What was her fascination with melancholy? We didn't believe that one should allow sadness to get the better of them, it was wrong. Of course, you'd have to be made of stone not to feel it, but she never let it go: it was the kind of sadness that crosses boundaries, that lurks within your soul forever, that sweeps you gently along like a breeze, step by step.

Sandra cried in front of a john. The john got angry and hit her with the back of his hand. The blow hurt Sandra's face and so did the malice behind it. Her face crumpled up in sadness. Her boyfriend hit her too, in the pit of her stomach, for letting herself get hurt, for letting the moon hold sway forever. Sandra's sadness meant that she was forever plagued by violence. How many times have I written that word in these pages?

I too have wandered the city, not knowing what to do, where to hide. Because love never came. My youth was slipping through my fingers and love never came. I suffered on account of it. I also suffered from rejection. But the absence of love is the worst part. The solution: thirty pills, a few anticonvulsants, and a letter to my parents. When I felt my strength slipping away, the strength to exist in our own way, something inside me went to my housemates for help. A surge of defiance, I thought. Because death lurks in weakness.

What a coward, a cowardly, dark prostitute. Cowardice is such a turnoff. The cry that had welled up inside me was authentic, my body wasn't ready to die. I'll never again be tempted to end it all. Now it's simply a gentle death wish that visits every now and again with a bourgeois languor that shames me.

Travestis hang themselves, travestis slit their wrists. Travestis continue to suffer after death, from the curiosity of gawkers, police investigations, gossiping neighbors, the still-warm, creamy blood on the bed.

SANDRA FELT SORRY for another woman in the Park: a tramp who lived underneath the Banco Provincia on Bajada Pucará, a bum with a pack of dogs, plenty of wool, and the ability to indulge in hours of contemplation from the excellently positioned post she had staked out for herself. The place where she'd set up her yellow-and-purple tent gave her a view of the dying sun in the west while she smoked her pipe and fed her dogs, leaning on the cart she needed to get around, because her obesity had gummed up her legs. Silvia the diabetic, mother of dogs and friend of travestis. The woman we went to visit every morning when they amputated her legs. The clatter of our high heels made the hospital windows shudder. The doctors were grateful for our color, our costume jewelry, our shrill-smelling perfumes, for lifting their patients' spirits during their slow, quiet farewells. Silvia's admittance had been serendipitous, she suffered a heart attack that would have taken her over to the other side if Sandra hadn't happened to be passing at that very moment, three in the morning, with a bottle of wine. She'd have died on the spot but would have kept her legs. Auntie Silvia liked to tell us that she'd given up on everything, she was sick of it all. But not any more. She died of pneumonia the same winter they took her legs. A virus she'd caught in the hospital, they said. We found out when we went to visit her one morning. It was like she'd decided to die in the hospital instead of recovering as she was supposed to. As she wheezed and coughed up bubbles of blood, she asked for her dogs and told the nurses to let us know. She wanted us to keep their place for them. To set up a warm bed and put out water and food every day. We kept our word and looked after her dogs as best we could. They latched on to us naturally, shrugging off their orphanhood. We split up the duties among ourselves, feeding them with our leftovers. After all, we were the city's leftovers too. The bitches came over and licked our hands, some got edgy and looked as though they were going to bite us, but the others drove them away so they wouldn't get our clothes dirty. Often was the time they saved us from a beating. They'd appear out of nowhere whenever tension was in the air. And then they simply returned to the tent of the woman who had taken them in. Every now and again they had puppies who left once they'd been weaned.

———

BY THE END of the winter, Auntie Encarna had started to play a dangerous game. We all warned her but were cowed by her fierce determination. We didn't know how to tell her that it wasn't a good idea to expose herself in the neighborhood in broad daylight without pissing her off. Encarna went out shopping with the boy in the pram. She said she had no choice, she had to walk with him in sunlight. To sit in a square and watch him sleep. To show her son to the world, the child she'd found in a ditch. But to ordinary people on the street, it was a disturbing sight. Sometimes we went out with her so she wouldn't be alone but that made things worse, it was an added danger, just one more on top of all the others we faced already. Men looked at Auntie Encarna very strangely, and the women were worse. She had the boy in her arms and Maria the Mute walked next to her with a backpack on her shoulder filled with everything Twinkle needed. They'd sit in the plaza and shroud themselves with their cloaks of invisibility. The weather was fair, the sun began to warm Encarna's skin, her shaved, made-up cheeks.

"He's my nephew," Auntie Encarna would tell the more inquisitive. "My sister's son from Formosa. She's in a wheelchair so I take him out myself." When people asked about the father, she'd say: "The father? He went to try his luck in Spain."

At first everyone believed her because during the economic crisis everyone went to Spain. But then they'd look at her large hands and made-up face, openly inspecting her. Until Maria stood up and hurried them back home to make sure that that was as far as things got.

Then one day the man at the newspaper kiosk called us faggot childnappers. Auntie Encarna asked Maria to take Twinkle in Her Eye for her. Then she walked over to the kiosk, leaned over the counter, and grabbed the man by his greasy shirt.

"When Monsignor Quarracino said that faggots and trannies should go off to live on an island somewhere, we should have listened. But fools that we are, we stayed," she growled, her face very close to his. The kiosk owner was so scared that he started to snivel and offer up cowardly apologies.

ONE DAY we went to sunbathe on Duck Island in Alberdi. We wore miniskirts and short tank tops or just our bras. We lay on the grass and rubbed Coca-Cola over our bodies to get better tans. We were covered in sugar and attracted bees. We were the flowers of Duck Island.

No, there's no getting away from it: we were nocturnal by nature. We avoided daylight. The sun weakened us, it exposed our skin issues, our five o'clock shadow, the undeniable features of men who weren't us. We didn't like to go out in the daytime because the masses would rebel against these revelations, they'd hound us with insults, they wanted to shackle and lynch us in plazas. The open disdain, the brazen way they stared at us. We don't like to go out in the daytime because honorable society women, ladies with professional hairdos and fine wool cardigans, would be scandalized and denounce us. They'd point their harpy fingers at us and turn us into pillars of salt, quick to collapse, an avalanche of loose cells falling apart like pearls from a broken necklace. We didn't like going out in the daytime because we weren't used to it, we couldn't adapt to the corset of their restrictions. Better to sleep in, locked in our rooms, watching TV or just doing nothing.

We did nothing during the day, we banished ourselves from productive society. But that afternoon we decided to get some sun. The first warm, sunny days, the first heat, flirting with chongos, a tit gone astray, letting the carnivorous eye of a nipple slip out, the music at full blast, ice creams bought from a vendor who said we were beautiful, conversations with the Peruvian woman who came to lie down next to us, who was also sunbathing but fully clothed.

We were there to be written about. To be immortalized.

That day the streets were quiet. We were the only ones in the whole city. Anyone who saw us that afternoon lying on the grass, drinking maté in the sun, covered in Coca-Cola, a liquid caramel color, would have dreamed of our bodies and laughter, it would have been an unbearable sight, like a vision of God.

IT'S THE HEAT, the maddening heat. Having spent so many years suffering in hellfire, the obligatory siestas when you'd pretend to have a cool, invisible house with curtains in the windows that keep out the heat of the bush. It was so hot that Mommy was afraid we'd melt in the haze. We took our nap sweating like animals, alone, with no energy for anything.

Taking turns to fetch water from a communal spigot; you couldn't drink the well water any more. It was so hot in the village that everything went bad: the water, the earth, the food, hearts and souls. Heat still makes me angry. Travesti heat was no different. Caked makeup that got sticky, a mask of warm mud blocking up the pores so that our souls wouldn't slip out every time we were attacked. Our faces turned into a mask, the most beautiful of all masks, travesti features more authentic than our actual ones, conceived for another world, a better world where such masks are possible.

Meanwhile we were Indians in war paint, beasts who stalked the Park at night, on the lookout for the unwary. We were always angry, brutish in our tenderness, unpredictable, crazy, resentful, poisonous. We were forever ready to burn the whole place down: our parents, friends and enemies, the middle classes with their comforts and routines, the posh kids who all looked the same, the patrician cocksuckers who scorned us so, our running masks, the anger painted on our skin protesting a world that looked the other way, that protected itself at the expense of ours, sucking life from us just because it had more money. So we chased our johns, forced into heat, into feeling that there was nothing worse than being a fairy choking on the hot world of men, where all issues are resolved with kicks and punches. Forced into the secret wish to kill them all, to end the world once and for all, to see if that would also sate our anger over the abuse to which we had all been subjected. Perhaps that was why we stole from them. Not much: twenty, fifty pesos slipped out of a wallet, nothing. No families were going to go hungry because of it. It was just a gesture. I'm young and believe I have a right to do this. That the money belongs to me because I'm at a disadvantage in this scene we share, the john and I. Later, at home, they'd notice the loss, missing the money that I'd already spent on one of the small pleasures that illuminate the lives of the poor. At the time, I went to the movies a lot. Sometimes I'd buy a book. Sometimes I had enough for a nightdress. I learned from the other travestis, it was a trick of the trade and inevitable, given the pittance they paid for our bodies and talents. It wasn't a tip because it was taken without consent. But it was still legitimate, payment to compensate for the unseen violence of every trick we turned. Our entire existence was a crime. I was a five-foot-two thief, picking pockets at light speed, while they were asleep or in the bathroom. You needed to learn fast: if you dithered too long, if the john came out of the bathroom to find you messing around with his wallet, he'd hit you. But if you just acted without a second thought, you had plenty of time. I was pretty good at it, until one day a john sent me a text message: "Did you steal money from my wallet?"

"I'm a whore, not a thief," I answered. I didn't really know what I meant by that. He never came back, which was a pity, because he was handsome. But he deserved it, just like all the rest. They need to understand that we're more expensive than their heterosexual minds can comprehend.

THE NIGHT OF my birthday was the hottest of the year. I decided not to work, but I did stop by to say hello to a few of my colleagues. On the way, a john made me a lovely offer and I accepted. When I was done I went to look for them in their usual spot and found that they were surrounded by a caravan of students celebrating the fact that one of them had graduated. Pretty boys dressed as travestis in one of those obscene four-by-four trucks their parents buy with money flogged from the backs of the poor. They were all drunk, celebrating and screaming the worst insults you can think of at us. Meanwhile they showered us in beer, drove off, circled the Park, and came back for another round of abuse. There weren't many of us and we began to get more and more nervous, sensing that this wouldn't end well. We decided to take refuge behind the carousel, and get something cool to drink from one of the carts, staying quiet and trying not to let our frustration show. I asked out loud: "Wouldn't you just love to kill them all?" Angie answered: "I'd fuck them with a red-hot iron first." Sandra nodded, muted by impotence and fear.

It was the anger that had embedded itself in each of us. We longed to tear the city down. To put an end to all the worlds outside of our own, the only true world. To poison their food, ruin their gardens with their neatly mowed lawns, boil the water in their pools, smash up their shitty trucks, rip their gold chains from their necks, take hold of their pretty, well-fed faces and rub them into the asphalt until we'd ground right through to the bone.

I wonder what would have happened if, rather than suppressing the anger, shoving it right down into our travesti souls, we'd have organized. But what happened instead? Where did just swallowing the poison lead us? Into early

graves. With the exception of the odd sudden fratricidal out-
break, travestis wouldn't hurt a fly.

RIGHT FROM THE FIRST MOMENT I stepped
inside Auntie Encarna's house, I thought it was paradise. I
was used to hiding my true identity in the boardinghouses
where I'd lived before, suffering like a bitch with my thing
choking inside panties one size too small. But in the pink
house travestis wandered naked through a patio overflowing
with plants, talking openly about the effects of silicon gel,
giggling as they shared their shameful hopes and dreams,
comparing their bruises from nights when they'd been in the
wars, maté straws stained with lipstick, the smell of armpit
and perfume, the television constantly blaring Brazilian
soap operas, airing awful childhood memories that left you
as exposed as a newborn lying in the snow. It wasn't uncom-
mon for one of us to suddenly choke up and withdraw only to
return later fully clothed and ready to sin.

One afternoon, when I was still a new arrival, we were
drinking maté and giggling while they taught me how to
cover my beard with white soap, told me about the hormones
I should be taking, and the safest places to inject yourself
with aircraft oil, when suddenly the door to the street opened
with a bang and a group of well-built travesti Amazons came
in carrying a bloody comrade. I suggested that we call the police, but the girls knew better and decided to deal with her
themselves, out of sheer love. The victim's boyfriend had

found out that he was HIV positive and that she'd given it to him, so he'd taken his anger out on her until she'd passed out.

Under the blood, bruising, and broken teeth, there was a beautiful girl. I knew her. She came from the same valley as me. But she was in a bad way, the boyfriend had given her a real beating. Her face was a mess, her ears were bleeding, and she could barely breathe through her broken ribs. She was racked with terrifying shudders and convulsions. We travestis cried as we cared for her, this shitty world was too full of evil and brutality, too full of senseless injustice, our paths were too strewn with misery. The pain of one of our number was shared by us all. We cried like poorly paid mourners and tried to clean what could be cleaned with iodine and alcohol. While we were at it La Machi arrived, a medicine woman who was rumored to be able to bring the dying back to life with black magic she'd learned in Brazil.

She was a sparse-haired travesti, apparently incapable of making herself look presentable, but she was so tough that we could have used her as a ram to batter down the walls of the cathedral. La Machi shooed us to one side while our friend writhed in pain. Although she was clearly drunk, her teeth were stained with lipstick, and the little hair she had left stank of smoke, we stood aside for La Machi and dutifully bit our tongues. We'd put the patient in Auntie Encarna's bed, she'd taken the baby into the kitchen and was now sitting with him there to shield him from the nasty side of life.

La Machi began to talk to someone we couldn't see. "I'm praying to the Virgin because she's a woman and understands us," she said, rearranging the patient's hands while she let out a screech that ran right through our bodies and tightened our sphincters. La Machi prayed, running her hands over the body like she was trying to read it. Every time one of us made the slightest noise, she stared at us furiously and went on praying in her language. When the first gag reflex came, she called for cloths and cold water. Then she took out a foul-smelling cigar from the bag that hung at her waist and started to smoke, looking down at the patient, as though she were taking her time to size up the demon inside of her, deciding how best to vanquish it.

From the same bag at her waist, she took out a piece of dried meat, nibbled it with the few teeth she had left, and started to recite something in a very quiet, intense voice as she inhaled and blew the smoke and ashes over the patient, who coughed and moaned weakly, like a sheep with its throat slit. La Machi was absorbed in her ritual and we didn't know what to do beyond passing a bottle of wine from hand to hand. Even though it was a warm afternoon, we were shivering. Cold had lodged itself in our minds. Someone offered to put the kettle on and someone else said "Oh yes!" as though just waking up from a nightmare. La Machi told us angrily to shut up and went on praying and praying until she let out a powerful burp. The prayers grew more and more intense along with the burping and gagging, it was hard to tell whether this was an act or she really believed in all this exorcism business, the patient could barely breathe from the pain. Then La Machi took a deep breath, her eyes rolled into the back of her head and she spit out the piece of meat she'd been chewing, which was now a black, viscous substance, and started to scream: "There it is! There's the one that has caused so much pain! The evil creature, the snake!" I thought to myself that the only snake that hurt us was our yearning for a dick inside of us, a dick to fill and satisfy us, that demanded our money and hit us because that was just how sordid we were.

La Machi stamped the piece of meat into the ground. Then suddenly, she stopped and said that now only the most exhausting part remained: the work of taking care of the patient. She went into the kitchen, found a dustpan and brush and cleaned up the mess before leaving us alone with the victim. Her work was done. What was left was the magic of travestis: cleaning the wounds with a cloth and warm water, swaddling her in blankets, doing her hair, and singing quietly. A very mundane kind of magic. The kind anyone might work, but seldom does.

JUST AFTER I turned fifteen, I tied a knot in the giant T-shirt that was part of my disguise as the boy my parents wanted, and placed my newly svelte torso on display for all to see. I wore the T-shirt with a pair of very tight shorts from my recent childhood, forerunner of what was to come, the faggot I was to be, the precocious travesti, the horny teenager. I didn't really know what to do with my sexuality, I was completely disoriented and had no one to talk to, so I began to experiment, dissecting my body, exploring it piece by piece. I rode my bike to the outskirts of town, the road where trucks passed by. I spent my childhood perched on the flanks of that bike, it was like a chrome dragon swooping through the morning air, showing off a body I'd never get back, making myself into an object, into valuable flesh, to live the only life that was available in that town, my whole existence dedicated to an abundance of clandestine sensuality. That was already who I was, it was already what I was into. Giving hand jobs to teamsters in the cabins of trucks parked askew by the side of the road, grabbing fistfuls of small bills, already versed in the art of deceit, pretending to be older, pretending to be a woman, listening to their pleading, saying please and then going off in search of another and another and another. A teenage girl climbing into trucks to learn something about life. That is who I was. Who I am.

———

THEN THERE WAS the other life, the legitimate life, daylight life lived among heterosexuals with light skin and good manners. University life, which occurred behind the night's back. The gray routine with which I clung to respectability, my dull neighbors, the students I saw every day. Going to the supermarket, to classes, and even to parties where my travesti experience was inconceivable. The attempts to adjust, the effort to make myself into a chameleon, to fit in, to have their lives. For people to like me, to be reserved, friendly, smart, committed, hardworking, to meet the demands of a life for which I wouldn't be condemned or judged. Always alert, always watching out for myself.

Trips back home to visit my parents as a humble, obedient son. No makeup, my hair pulled back, in a baggy hoodie and sweatpants, backpack slung over my shoulder and sunglasses to avoid unwanted eye contact. The prodigal son returning home to a mother and father who wanted to see me living the life of the little man who had claimed my body without my consent. They had wiped the aberration from their minds, they'd completely switched off and in return I had to play my part, fulfill my obligation, pay my dues: I was not to dress as a woman.

It was a double life. The journey to see my parents across the sierras, the nausea, the ceaseless urge to give up on everything, the tumult of feelings, the uncertainty over whether I loved or hated them, whether I could continue living by their rules in exchange for their love and affection or whether I was going to end up drowning in resentment and suffering.

The constant comparisons. Interacting with my fellow students and professors, trying every day to continue the decorous farce. Envying the haircuts of my female fellow students, their bodies, their vaginas, their boyfriends, their relationships with their families. Lusting after men who rejected me for who I was. I couldn't admit that I was a prostitute because a travesti prostitute was the worst aberration you could think of. Writing in the middle of the night, after I'd come back from my nightly round, listening to La Negra Vernaci's radio program, which gave me support and company in my lonely rented room. Coffee and a joint. Clandestine visits from a lover. College notes on a table, trying to read, to understand, but it was impossible, just like I couldn't hope to attend all my classes if I wanted to make enough money to live on. The daily disintegration of my optimism and intentions, a battle I always lost, the obligation to visit my parents every now and again. My friends, the travestis with whom I'd formed a family, couldn't understand how I put up with it, the exposure, the daylight, the glare of the heterosexual gaze, how I could study and take exams with professors who had absolutely no idea of my nocturnal existence.

The life in which I was always an outsider, owner of nothing, visiting the world of the normals, my straitlaced, middle-class fellow students, the mountain of secrets and lies that I had to keep from them. A shitty life, in which your desires were forever repressed. But it was what made the other life possible: my night life, the one in which I had sex for money, where I lusted after men.

And so I learned to lie, to hide my secret, to protect myself from inquiring gazes, my parents, my friends, my professors, the guardians of the truth who demanded purity of the flesh and submission of the spirit. I was perfectly capable of telling them that I was just as well adjusted as they were, in fact I was better, because I could be like them and how I wanted to be at the same time. And they would applaud with relish because they thought their model of the world was perfect, they'd open the doors of their homes and invite me in so I could see their hypocrisy up close.

I saw the sofas on which they rested their exhausted bodies, the drawers in which they kept the cash to pay for their children's private school, beach vacations, and their wives' jewels. But I also saw them come to the Park in their brand-new cars, just as willing to pay for a woman with a penis. Nothing thrilled them more: "It drives me crazy to see you sleeping with that knife between your legs."

Which is just how hypocritical they are, just like us, the desperate travestis perfectly willing to never say a word in exchange for money. Which is why it's so simple to lie. Why you quickly learn to say what the other wants to hear. I lied to my customers and lied at college and lied when I went to visit my parents who only really cared about one thing, every parent's dream: to have a son with a respectable profession.

———

SOMETIMES I'd be very tired after work. I felt that I was wearing out my body at a terrible pace. It was like what Doña Rosita the Spinster said: every year that passed was like having another item of underwear torn from your body. Premature aging began to manifest itself in the form of exhaustion. As though the dark god who had given me a handful of beauty was now opening up that hand and letting it slip through its fingers like sand. Every winter night, when I collapsed into bed after my nightly rounds, I felt a tiredness very similar to death. And I didn't even work every night. I confess it: I wasn't a good prostitute. I had to be in dire economic straits to go to bed with a john I didn't like. I had to be mired in debt to agree to get into a car belonging to someone I wasn't completely sure about. I didn't do it following a professional routine, my schedule was determined by need. I don't know from whom I inherited that lack of ambition, why I was so comfortable with living hand to mouth, but I didn't like working every night. My prostitute existence was governed by a very simple rule: if I needed money, my body was right there ready to earn it. If bread was already on the table, then I could stay at home like a bearded angel.

But poverty draped its cloak further and further over me. The owner of the boardinghouse's threats to start charging rent, everything I spent on shampoo, makeup, clothes, shoes, and medicine when I got sick, all determined how often I went out. But life was also made more complicated by the haggling of tricks willing to pay fortunes for their cars, clothes, or smartphones without blinking an eye but who'd argue with a travesti over the price of her body long enough for their haircuts to go out of style.

And so I squandered the little beauty that had been given to me in about two or three years. Beauty was fleeting. Wonderful while it lasted, but the poor diet, sleepless nights, alcohol, and cocaine chiseled away at a once gorgeous physique. It began to grow difficult to charge the same as my colleagues for the wreck it had become. I wasn't an old-school travesti with massive tits or a face that had had work done to it. I was a small-town travesti whose fate it was to have a diminutive body, tiny size-five feet, and a very feminine voice. "Your voice," the other travestis would say to me, "I so envy your voice."

So, tired after fucking one, two, three johns, I still had to go home and get rid of the smell of other people, the bitter expression that came with placing myself on display like a piece of flesh on the butcher counter and having to put up with the disappointment or regret of a customer. "You're hairy, ugly, and dark," said one as the car pulled away, honking like a crazy man. Then there was the wait, later, back at the boardinghouse. Waiting for the man I was obsessed with, the man who won't read this book. Waiting for him to knock at my window at five, six, seven in the morning, a little tipsy or completely wasted with sexual demands I never dared refuse him.

Sometimes he'd complain and make scenes because he'd arrived early and listened from the street while I pleasured a john. I was exhausted, I had long since misplaced the divine energy with which I'd previously popped up like a jack-in-the-box every morning, but I'd still rush to open the door and make love to him. And for real: with love, kisses, barefaced, without my stuffed bra or hiding my penis, and without using it like a sword either.

We were young, we were able to love multiple times throughout the early hours. We were able to love until we hated one another. He was the passion that distorted my life. I couldn't not want him, even though he could be aggressive and even violent, with him I was how I wanted to be. In spite of my crippling exhaustion, which came with having been constantly afraid since childhood, with him I embraced my role as slave, as an object. I adopted that way of living even though I was tired and afraid. Simply because I was rewarded by his body, especially his body inside mine, the proof of his desire for me, for my femininity. And so I submitted meekly, I was less than a whore, much less than a whore: horribly befuddled by an idea of love. A relationship like that was an insult to my trade. And the love also shamed me in front of my college friends. How was my fistful of beauty ever going to last if I was so willing to plunge headfirst into such an ugly place?

I'D PLEASURED HIM at the boardinghouse several times. He was handsome and rude. He scorned me the way someone who's been handsome their whole lives does. Sometimes he was dirty and I had to ask him to take a shower. But he was good-looking, which was enough to take him on as a

customer. He worked for the municipality as a traffic monitor. He always wore beige, a reflection of his spirit. One day
he offered me triple the usual fee to shove the batteries from
my radio into my ass. It was a lot of money all at once and I
took it. I can't blame poverty for that. I can't offer any excuse
at all. All I can say is that I felt guilty for many years for having subjected myself to such a humiliation.

The guilt that gnawed away at me took years off my life
expectancy, until one afternoon I went to see Auntie Encarna
with tears streaming down my face. How could I look my parents or friends in the eye after that? Auntie Encarna, the boy
in her arms, wandered around the house ignoring me completely while I followed her like a lapdog, sick to my stomach
with guilt, bawling my eyes out. Until she stopped suddenly,
turned around, and slapped me with her free hand. "I'm sick
of the miserable way you look at yourselves!" she said, and
opened her blouse to free a breast that was almost as big as
the boy in her arms. Taking the nipple between her thumb
and forefinger, she squeezed and a dribble of milk beaded
like a tear. "Look: this is what's important." She buttoned her
blouse and slammed her bedroom door in my face, but not
before saying: "You won't be spending Christmas alone this
year. One of the girls from the Park is holding a barbecue at
home and we're all invited."

Oh, wet nurse Encarna of the miraculous breasts. Oh Difunta Correa with aircraft oil tits, saintly patron of all those
of us who found you in our ceaseless search for a mother, to
find a mother to console us on our nights of regret, a mother
to teach us not to suffer.

WHEN CHRISTMAS EVE came around, I had to take off my sandals and walk barefoot down a dirt street to get to our hostess's house. One of the girls was waiting at the end, hose in hand, giggling as she washed our feet. Every now and again she put the hose to her pubis, screaming "I came loose!"

Being invited to the home of another travesti is a lovely occasion because it allows you to see what you have in common and where you differ. It's how we build our identity, our future home. There could be no better mirror. The Christmas table had been carefully laid. Plastic mats, stainless steel cups, and some old wineglasses to one side which were only to be used for the toast at midnight. Old folk music from the nineties was playing, reminding me of Christmases at my grandmother's house while the smell of roasting meat wafted in through the window. The only other sign of Christmas was the wreath at the door. No further decoration was needed because we were all like Christmas trees, decked out in our best outfits, a little out of vanity and a little to keep poverty at bay. Observers would never imagine the modesty of our everyday lives because we were all dressed like royalty. The menu was barbecued chicken with cold mayonnaise salad. The nougat, pan dulce, peanuts, and everything else I had always hated about Christmas tasted delicious that night. The hostess's mother treated us like her daughters. At one point, she led me by the hand into her bedroom and rummaged in her chest of drawers before taking out a vintage shift in perfect condition: "Here, this is for you, you're so skinny, it'll look good on you."

At one point during dinner, one of the girls made a joke at the expense of another who'd had an operation and now had a perfect vagina. The girl who'd undergone the procedure was asked whether she'd had two in there at the same time yet, and I asked two whats, and they all laughed and made fun of me for pretending to be naive until I confessed that I'd never seen a newly built vagina. They all started to chant, "Get it out! Get it out! Get it out!" and the owner of the brand-spanking-new vagina lifted her dress, tucked it under her chin and pulled her thong to one side to show me her pussy.

We laughed for a good long time. I thought it was a beautiful vagina and she spread the lips wide so we could appreciate it in all its splendor. It had cost her plenty and she was justly proud. Then we all danced. One of the girls whom we called Thalia, because she had a waist like a violin, dropped a full bottle on the floor but nobody minded. We took turns dancing with the mother of the hostess, then it was time for the toast, sparklers, and fireworks, we were deafened by the neighborhood display. The hostess gave each of us gifts, a scarf with our initials, which she'd sewn herself, making us all feel like members of the most exclusive club in the world. We apologized for not bringing gifts of our own but she insisted it didn't matter.

Then they all started giving me advice about how to enhance my feminine features and praised my voice because it was so womanly. One asked me to sing and I sang the one about the bull in love with the moon, then another started to cry and the others made fun of her when she said, "It's just that I miss my daddy." We got drunker and drunker and did the dishes and sat outside in the little garden, eaten alive by the mosquitoes, lighting coils under the loungers and toasting again and again for everything that occurred to us. One of the girls said that she'd like her brother to finish secondary school and another said that she'd like to save up some money to make her butt a little bigger, and they asked me what I wanted and I said nothing, so they told me to wish for something perfect and I had no idea what to say. Strength, I thought, but I was ashamed to say so. Then we all went quiet to listen to the neighbors fucking. One of the girls cried out that they should invite us, it was a lovely night for it. And so the first rose-colored clouds snuck up on us, signaling that it was time to go home, and we went out onto the muddy street with our shoes in one hand. One headed out toward the airport to get the bus, another went home, which was nearby, and I got into a car with a very drunk gentleman from Rio Ceballos and we ended up making love in a turnout watching the planes take off and land, carrying last-minute passengers who must have celebrated Christmas on the plane. I'd put on the old shift and the john, after paying, invited me to breakfast at a little stand by the airport. I told him about the travestis' Christmas and also that I'd seen a surgically created pussy for the first time and that that night I'd made a decisive break with God. Drunk as he was, he said, "Good for you."

———

TWO NIGHTS LATER, a john got angry with me because I couldn't get an erection to penetrate him. I could barely get my whole body upright after nights flogging it on the street. I was always on the verge of collapse, always drunk, like my father coming back from his nightly booze sessions. I wasn't ashamed to walk around like that, smelling of alcohol, sweating alcohol, with that egotistical wit that alcohol gives you. But I couldn't get an erection. The john, who had already paid for a two-hour slot at the hotel, and was afraid that someone he knew might see me with him, got angrier and angrier. He started to bark violent insults. This wouldn't get me anywhere, I was taking work from people who could do it properly, a cock like that and you don't know how to use it, what a shame, what the hell kind of whore are you, you've got no tits and a mustache to boot, how had he been stupid enough to take this disease-ridden, long-haired coon back to the hotel? Several times he threatened to hit me and I gulped and listened without moving a muscle on my face. I was afraid, but it was also funny to see him so desperate to get fucked, he was a spoiled little boy pleading for cock. His anger and my drunkenness made our efforts pointless, who knows what I'd taken that night. He could scream bloody murder as long as he wanted, my dick wasn't going to react. What made him angriest was the fact that now we had to leave together, in front of the concierge at the shitty hotel that I wasn't fit to set foot in, you fuck dark whores like me in the dark, I was worthless. Then he demanded that I pay for half.

He wouldn't come to his senses, livid over the fact that I couldn't give him what he wanted, even though I'd offered a thousand other options. He insulted me all the way from the room to the car, but I was so drunk I barely noticed. It was a long way home but there was a chance that another unsuspecting lamb might fall into the clutches of the she-wolf.

I was walking back down Deán Funes, the city was at rest, the only places open were cyber cafés. The open doors had bad breath, from inside came laments crying out to be heard, only agonized ghosts occupied cyber cafés at that hour, the doors were open because of the heat, the tobacco smoke hovering thick like storm clouds over the heads of the cybernauts, a lot of lonely people, people who just want to talk about something, it didn't matter what so long as it was with somebody, even if it was just via chat, to say something and be read, to lie even, but to talk, to make contact with someone.

Along the way, I came across a local duchess, Vale, the same woman who up until a few months ago had shouted "Faggot!" at me every time I passed by. Today Vale came over to me enveloped by the smell of whiskey, dressed in a red vinyl jacket and wearing fuchsia extensions. In this city she was as inexplicable, unsettling, damaging, and sweet as Coca-Cola. She was complaining about hard times with uncharacteristic vulnerability. She hadn't picked up anyone for two or three days.

"How's it going for you?" she asked, and I told her what had just happened, the john who'd left in a huff because I couldn't fuck him. She collapsed in peals of laughter and asked if I was taking hormones, but I said I wasn't. Then she told me that she had the answer: a little Viagra pill would solve everything. She took part of a blister from her handbag, split one of the pills in two with her nail, and told me to take half to see how it went. We laughed at the situation right there on the corner of Deán Funes and Fragueiro, it really was absurd.

"All that effort to turn yourself into a travesti and you end up banging faggots."

Then she started asking potential customers whether they were passive and told the ones who were to move along. From her throne, the porch where she stood, she'd cry out: "The guy in the red car is passive!" and double over laughing. But then someone arrived on a bicycle and they settled on a price for an hour and went into her little apartment with the bike and everything. I continued on my way home, with half a Viagra pill sitting in my purse like a slumbering frog.

I DECIDED TO TAKE IT the next day. At first, everything went well. I debuted it with a slightly beige, insipid tennis player who, when mounted, started to buck like an angry horse and beg and plead like another person entirely, as though the first thrust had changed his entire personality. He paid up and left. The problem was that the erection didn't go along with him. The next john wanted nothing to do with being passive, in spite of what they say about people from Córdoba, and neither did the next, so I was wandering the Park in exasperation, alone. Everyone else had gone off somewhere so my only company was my painful erection. I'd never had one like it. There I was, like an incontinent, brutish stud, suffering from an affliction that was both embarrassing and somewhat dishonorable for a deeply submissive dom like me. I covered up the evidence of my tumescence with my coat and went home, but I couldn't sleep. Just when the effect seemed to be wearing off, when I'd relaxed and begun to get drowsy, the least touch would set it off again. So I jacked off, again and again, until I was exhausted. I went through a mental parade of all my lovers, allowing them to take turns in the forefront of my memory. I spent hours and hours with my dick in my hand, the dark object of desire over which the johns got so angry, throwing tantrums, kicking, screaming, and begging, you should see how these unsatisfied husbands beg for the penis I had in my hand, rubbing it up and down to get rid of the effect of the damn pill. You should see how these family men who bust their humps to feed their wife and children beg for it. You should see how they yearn in the silence of the night dreaming of the penis I was squeezing and choking with gritted teeth. You should see how they plead to take it in their mouths and shove it deep inside their asses, to feel what it's like to be penetrated by a woman, to know that it's a woman causing them this pain, arousing their lust. You should see how their values go to hell when they have this penis inside of them. Why, then, do we think that it's our fault we can't make them brave enough to stay, or leave forever or at least not to infect us with their fear?

It was several painful hours before the effects wore off. In the end I wanted nothing to do with it, I was ready to cut it off, to tear it out with my teeth just to put an end to the erection. But the next day, it also gave me a good laugh, an unforgettable fit of the giggles, I could barely catch my breath. Viagra nights are legendary among us travestis. Every night one of us experiences one, she then tells her friends and they tell all their friends and friends of friends, pissing themselves the whole time. Damnable Viagra, curse of Priapus.

I WAS SITTING in the pharmacy, waiting my turn alongside a bunch of old people also in the queue. We had a lot in common. Perhaps the only difference between them and me was their youthful spirit: they were clearly more jovial than I was. Everything that made me unique, every grain of beauty, had died somewhere out there on the street. One of the old men asked a question at the counter before coming over to sit next to me. As he did so the air trapped in his clothes billowed out, flowing into my nose and also that of the lady on the other side. We both grimaced: piss and ammonia, like my grandfather at the end.

Suddenly she strode in, tall as a cornstalk and just as skinny, with sunglasses covering her eyes and features. Auntie Encarna used to say, "All travestis possess the gift of transparency and the ability to dazzle." We were all used to walking very fast, almost cantering along. Our speed was a function of our need to be transparent. Every time our humanity solidified, men and women, children, the elderly, and teenagers would cry out that we weren't transparent at all, we were travestis, we were everything that moved them to spout insults, that they found disgusting. So, to greater or lesser effect, we opted for transparency. The triumph of getting home while managing to stay invisible and safe from attack. Transparency, camouflage, invisibility, and visual silence were our small daily joys. Moments of rest.

And so now she came into the pharmacy, subtly declaring that she was alive. She was wearing baggy jeans and sunglasses and was tall and thin in a way I could only dream of. I knew she was trying to go unnoticed from the little details, the slope of her shoulders, her voice. And I was sorry that it wasn't working. Behind the counter there were the same old employees, exchanging glances. One immediately said something to the other, who snickered. One of the shopgirls came over to see what was so funny and joined in the mockery. Not content with reveling in their malice behind the counter, they looked to get the customers involved, and their invitation was accepted more than willingly: suddenly everyone was staring at the travesti who had tried to visit the pharmacy incognito. She noticed the half-stifled giggles, the murmuring, and got uncomfortable. She bowed her head, put on headphones, and sat down to wait. I saw it all. I watched my sister, my friend, my family, grow tired of the mocking eyes and leave without buying what she needed. I too was in a hurry and was running out of steam. I couldn't summon the energy to make the fuss that these nasty slaves to propriety deserved. I was so embarrassed by them. And I was so ashamed of myself for not doing justice and telling them all to go to the most stinking hell on earth. Children of shit piled upon shit, doing the shittiest thing imaginable. What do they know about the hours lost practicing the difficult art of transparency and dazzlement? "We're like a sunset seen without sunglasses," Auntie Encarna used to say. "Bright enough to blind you, to bewitch and frighten whoever looks at us." It's true, but we can always leave too. And our bodies go with us. Our bodies are our homeland.

ANGIE WAS THE PRETTIEST travesti of the Park. I'd never seen a travesti as beautiful as her in my entire life and I never saw her like again. She was tall, thin, always full of life, and always moving, like bamboo in the wind. I never found out how old she was, she was one of those travestis who never reveal their secrets. Her youthful beauty was complemented by the wisdom of an old soul, which hovered over her like an aura. When I met her she hadn't had any work done. She plucked her eyebrows a lot, making them very fine, the way people had them in the eighties. She had short hair and was so graceful that men called her Araceli. And they were right: she was just as beautiful as the actress Araceli González. You had to be very, very beautiful to have short hair if you were a travesti, the rest of us spent money we didn't have on wigs and extensions. But she wore her hair *à la garçon*, it never even got down over her ears, but that only made her more irresistible.

She went everywhere with her cousin, a sixteen-year-old fag who accompanied Angie on her rounds to get himself mounted among the trees in the Park. He gloated over his ability to make more money than us even though he wasn't a travesti. He waved his fistful of bills under our noses and declared that he was going to get an ice cream: "Anyone coming?" His cousin forced him to buy us all a cone at the ice cream place on Plaza España. We all showed off to one another, licking the ice cream like we were fellating Marlon Brando until some passerby said something mean and things got ugly, because we girls had short tempers.

They both lived in Alta Gracia. Every night they took the bus to the Park and every morning, as the sky turned red, they'd go back to their hometown. Angie was always in a rush because she had to make her boyfriend breakfast. He was a builder and went to work early. We'd met on the steps of the Park, one night when I went off to cry alone, the way I used to cry at the time. I was doing my thing when I heard a singsong laugh floating over toward me. It was them. They came down the stairs without looking at the steps, the way models walk in *Donna sotto le stelle*, that program on RAI. When they saw that I was alone at that hour, on the steps, they knew that they'd come across someone who needed cheering up.

The first words I heard come out of Angie's mouth were "I became a travesti because being a travesti is a celebration." It was her prescription for every ailment, it was how she lived. I guess she was born that way. Like a flower in the desert. "Oh no, darling, don't cry over a guy who gives you nothing. Being a travesti is a celebration, enjoy it." She was a rigorous follower of her own philosophy. She was always laughing, always generous and she always had candy in her pockets. She got me into the habit of sucking on mints during my work hours, not just because they helped with my marijuana, alcohol, and tobacco breath, but also because she said giving head to a john with a mint in your mouth made them love you more.

Her builder boyfriend regarded her profession with equanimity. They lived in Alta Gracia in a little house he'd built with his own hands, where Angie brought all her earnings. Angie worked hard and saved hard too. She was determined to live life to the full and had coupled up with the most wonderful Minotaur she could attract with a flutter of her eyelashes and her bewitching charm.

Her chongo was the most handsome we'd ever seen. He was dark with gray eyes and looked as though he was made of bricks. But that wasn't everything that made him desirable. He'd been out with travestis before and fought over more than once, occasionally with knives. People said he was hung like a mule and sweet as honey. I could tell that they were truly in love. And that Angie really was a celebration: beautiful, happy, unpredictable. It was impossible not to adore her. The Park had its queen.

When we asked her how she persuaded her chongo to accept what she did, Angie answered that she slept with other men the way he built houses for other families. Sometimes he came to pick her up and we'd shout "Bye, partner!" as though we shared the chongo between us, like we were all on the board of a limited company. Angie laughed and waggled her butt proudly because in a land racked by famine she was loved by someone who wore their heart on their sleeve.

One day her cousin and I had to be quick to interrupt a fight between her and another travesti. She'd found out that the evil little thing had been sending messages to her man and had come to demand satisfaction. But she didn't take into account the fact that the other woman was built like a circus strongman: the first punch knocked her down and she hit her head against a tree root. The other woman started kicking her on the ground. When we heard the screams we went over to break it up. I drew on all my rhetorical powers to calm the other travesti down. Once I'd finally managed to assuage her fury the bitch said, "Don't play crazy, honey, you don't know what kind of real crazy woman you might come across." I didn't like to see Angie all frightened and beaten up and neither did I enjoy accompanying her to the emergency room. She'd hit her head hard and was bleeding a little at the temple. Still, because we were always high on whiskey and clonazepam she was laughing, saying that her chongo would never sleep with a travesti with such a bushy mustache.

I only ever saw her cry once. She couldn't stand to cry or to see anyone else crying, and that was a problem because back then we travestis were real crybabies. Whenever one of us was sad, Angie would invite you out for a hot drink at a late-night café: "Being a travesti is a celebration, honey, look at all those people staring at us," she'd say pointing at the women looking at us in horror, like we were aliens. "They'd love to give what we do, darling. We give love." My heart skipped a beat because I adored Angie and admired the determination with which she went about her life.

One night, a couple of pretty boys, the kind you can never trust because no one that beautiful can have a good heart, invited us into their Renault Kangoo to party with them. I didn't like parties, it made me uncomfortable to have another travesti naked beside me, but because Angie did the talking I knew the money would be good and that we'd each do our job separately. It was about four in the morning on a Saturday night, a dangerous hour because the guys started to leave the nightclubs and bars and were wandering around drunk looking to transgress, to be the fastest in the West, to do some damage, to get their revenge on the world.

It was a dangerous time but it was also when the best kind of chongos you could hope for appeared: the single ones. We never wanted to miss out on the single men. Things always went well with them, it was as though good fortune really existed, as though Jesus' words had finally come to pass: the last had come first.

The middle of the night. We were stiff as Dante's statue and freezing, the kind of cold that made your back ache. The Kangoo pulled up in front of us and I saw the two golden princes in there, a little drunk, well dressed and scented, acting polite with money in their pockets. But after they'd got us into the back of their van and asked us to do everything a pair of sodomites like us could do, they refused to pay, saying they didn't pay for travestis.

Angie was very calm, saying in her sweetest voice that of course they were going to pay, darlings, because we'd been very open with them, we hadn't hidden a thing. But they claimed to feel scammed by a couple of faggots. I wanted to intervene with my rhetoric but one of the guys smacked Angie in the mouth and the other grabbed me by the throat and started to choke me. And so a real kerfuffle began, Angie reaching for the shiv in her jean pocket and me screaming like a crazy woman because I didn't think we'd get out of there alive, and amid the flurry of kicks and punches I saw the back of the Kangoo open up to let in the night sky, followed by Auntie Encarna, raised high on six-inch heels. She dragged the one choking me out of the van, then commenced to stomp on his balls with her high heels. In the confusion, Angie grabbed her shiv and stabbed the other one in the waist. I just sat and stared at my friend's beautiful, bloodied face and the mommy's boy sniveling and clutching his torso, but Auntie Encarna screamed, "Just get out of there, you idiots!" Then we saw a company of travestis riding to the rescue, ready to unleash all their pent-up anger.

ANGIE HAD MADE THE SHIV herself. It was a hotel soap bar with a razor attached to it with an elastic hair band. She could keep it in her sleeve, purse, or pocket. One night, she gave me one, saying, "Oh, my dear, you have no idea how good this coconut soap smells." She'd used it to cut a nasty gash in our attacker's waist the way Zorro cuts a Z in his enemies' shirts. That night, while we pressed ice-cold bottles of water against our wounds, Angie looked me in the eye and said, "Oh, my dear!" The blood on her teeth looked like smudged lipstick. Then she covered her mouth and leaned against me. When she was feeling better I walked her to the bus terminal and she said, "Thank you, honey," promising that on Sunday she'd have me around for a barbecue, her boyfriend would do the cooking.

ANGIE DIED of AIDS. Some of us watched her go. It was very quick, she turned green and skinny and left the Park. Her cousin gave me the awful news with a lackadaisical air I didn't appreciate at all: he said that he hadn't seen her since she was admitted to Rawson Hospital. Angie died holding her builder boyfriend's hand. He was with her the whole time. I went to visit her a couple of times before going to college and on both occasions I found him sitting on the steps, crying like a little boy. He was very young, I don't think he'd yet turned nineteen, and he was already a hop, skip, and jump from becoming a widower. One day he asked me for money to pay the electricity bill: he couldn't work and Angie's disease had eaten up their savings.

Auntie Encarna took Twinkle in Her Eye to see her so Angie could say goodbye but the nurses wouldn't let them in. They said it wasn't a good idea to bring the boy into the hospital, which was like a kind of emergency hotel for us, the anteroom to our mortality. "It's the only place where you belong," a policeman had said to me once while he was trying to arrest me. "That's where you'll end up," he said, pointing at the Rawson, our deathly flophouse.

The incident depressed me deeply. I was in a study group at college and the pretty girls I studied with would complain about banal problems I'd have loved to have had. It's not fair for a friend to die on you from the bug when you're just twenty years old.

Malicious gossips said that Angie's chongo went on to marry and have children with a girl. By then, the travestis in my pack had stopped lusting after him because they suspected she must have given it to him. Overnight he went from being a sex symbol we were all crazy about to being labeled an undesirable carrier. It was all very cruel. And in truth I never saw that lovely builder again but I am grateful to him, wherever he might be, for the love with which he treated my friend. I saw with my own eyes how he never let go of her hand during visiting hours and I also saw him on the steps, crumpled up in grief, drying his eyes with hands cured by lime. He had loved her the way sacred things in this world deserve to be loved. Because being with a travesti was a celebration for him too.

The Park wasn't the same without her, even though she didn't come every night when she was alive. Our routine went on as before, only it was more squalid now, our hip flasks were always at hand, we quarreled with johns and each other, cursing President De la Rúa and the pigs. And so we forgot the most important thing: that being a travesti is a celebration. The most beautiful of us all was no longer there to remind us.

THE TUMOR of our resentment. The bitterness of our orphanhood. The slow homicide committed against our species, the vixens, the she-wolves, the birds, the witches. I'm going to repeat myself even if it is a literary sin: the death wish. They were all very strong and came from an unknown, nameless place, the progenitor of our violence, at the back of our mind, where all was forgotten as we desensitized ourselves, part of the process that kept us alive day after day.

People would always say things about us: "Travestis are trouble," "Don't let a travesti into your home," "They're thieves," "They're difficult," "Poor things, it's not their fault they're that way." The disdain in their eyes. The way they insulted us. The stones thrown. The persecution. The police had pissed in Maria the Mute's eye while she was being held at gunpoint, telling her that if she didn't tell them her name, they'd unload the chamber into her head. With all of us looking on. All those beatings on top of the ones our parents had already given us, trying to change us back, to return us to the respectable world, the right way of doing things, to make us into people who form families and have children and love God and do their work diligently to make their bosses rich and grow old next to their wives. The fury at the silence and complicity of our mothers in the systematic degradation of our existence. Not even Twinkle in Her Eye could free us of a rage we would still carry with us like chains even when our lives were over.

WHEN THE NEIGHBORS began to call out "Pervert!" and "Childnapper!" as she passed by, Auntie Encarna started to go out less. She stayed locked up watching the Brazilian soap operas into which we sublimated our life stories. She stopped putting on makeup and began to slow down, like a pregnant dog. She'd lay her head over the boy's heart and speak to him in a language only they knew. Twinkle grew up enveloped in those secret whispered words, while from over the wall they called us diseased cocksuckers, trying to disrupt the peace Encarna had worked so hard to create. Sometimes we'd shout back, but that only made things worse. Once Abigail Cabelo de Fogo went to a window and opened her pants to show her enormous hairy cock to the scandalized neighbor with the face of an innocent grandmother who was waging her holy war against us. The next day someone wrote FAGGOTS on our door in massive letters in red spray paint. That obviously wasn't the old woman, which meant that the neighborhood was against us. We painted over it knowing that it was pointless, sooner or later it would reappear. The world of desire doesn't sparkle the way you might think.

HE WAS A HUNTER. He wore khaki pants and shirts and his muscular physique was a fair indication of what dangled between his legs. He was a friendly, virile animal who wore you out during sex, like you'd been wrestling with a bison. He'd broken several of our hearts because he wouldn't be tied down. He didn't speak much, wore a lot of scent, and was tender when he touched you. He worked as a security guard at the zoo and lived on his own in a small town, I can't remember which, on the outskirts of the city. It was rumored that he had a rottweiler that had killed a thief who broke in one night while he was working. When he was your trick you knew it would be a good night because he always paid the price you'd agreed on, he was clean, he knew how to treat a girl, he loaned us money, stroked us, urged us to drink less and take fewer drugs, and gave us tips. He covered all the costs and did so with humanity. A night with him was like the first date in a good relationship.

I knew that with him you had the right to feel good, really good, you could glean happiness from his body, however briefly. He took me to the zoo and we made love in the childcare center between little heart-shaped tables painted light blue and pink on cushions that the kindergarten teachers must have used to sit on when they played with the kids. After seeing him, I went straight home, I didn't need anything more. Sometimes he invited me on a walk around the zoo. We had to be quiet because the animals got sensitive at night. He had his flashlight and took me to where the lions were, looking at us with their glowing green eyes, pleading to be returned to the savanna. Or he'd take me to where the camels slept or let me listen to the cranes greet the dawn. Sometimes, in the middle of our walk, he got a sudden rush of blood and mounted me then and there, under the stars and among the animals. He took off all my clothes and all his and, nude in the open air, trying not to moan so as not to bother the animals, we did honor to sin.

The guard was a loner. He listened to Dolina's show on a portable radio and would sometimes give me unexpected gifts after ravaging me in the kindergarten. I was in love but he was more than twenty years older than me and the gossips said that he was married. I observed the nostalgia of the camels standing in front of the painted desert scene in their enclosure. It was like their keepers were making fun of them, I couldn't understand how they could be taken in, but the camels stared at it with a longing so full of wisdom that I was moved. The guard sometimes said, "If it was up to me, I'd open up the cages and let it all go to hell." I asked him why he didn't and he answered, "Because if I go to prison, you won't come to visit." Then I'd rub up against him like a horny dog. Even in front of the poor camels. The constellations can sometimes be very generous. My zoo guard gave me tenderness, brought me hot coffee on cold winter nights, and several times dropped me off at home in his car, saying goodbye with a kiss on the mouth.

MARIA THE MUTE was blacklisted everywhere. She wasn't allowed into bars, restaurants, or churches. They didn't even let her into filthy government offices. If she went to a supermarket she was asked to leave, when she went to the grocery she was driven away by their mocking. Poor Maria, the longest-suffering of us all, Twinkle in Her Eye's favorite, wasn't able to complain about her exile, but neither could she reconcile herself to the gray existence she was forced to put up with before reaching the promised land.

She was slowly turning into a bird with dark silver plumage. At first her deaf-mute chirping had a devastating power, you could hear her trying to communicate with someone halfway down the block. Then she decided to stay quiet so as not to scare the boy, because her language had all the bravado of a peacock's war cry. On nights of the full moon she kept Natali company during her voluntary incarceration and the two animals comforted one another, hidden away from the world, in an incomprehensible but rich, expressive, and bitter language.

We gave her all the support we could, we didn't know much but we were ready to help her through her terrifying mutation, her agonizing change. Victim of an unbreakable spell, she experimented with flight on the terrace, at night when no one could see her, and she grew smaller every day. She soon stopped eating cooked meals, she'd only peck at strips of raw meat while her nose turned into a long, elegant beak not unlike the golden cigarette holders you see in old Hollywood films. She covered herself with a blanket and walked around naked because her body had changed so much that no clothes would fit it.

We waited for months for her wings to grow stronger so she could fully unfurl them in the middle of the patio, but that didn't happen. She just grew claws where her feet had been and, strangers to good taste, we painted them bright red with glossy nail polish. Eventually she shrank into a little leaden bird that peered out from her nest in the lemon tree in the patio, watching Twinkle grow and chirping melancholy tunes that tore at your heart. Our bird, our freest sister, who could fly wherever she wanted. Maria the Bird, who ate worms and maggots from our palm. Now that I've spoken of her transformation, a part of me has died in the telling.

AFTER MARIA'S CHANGE, we went to Auntie Encarna's house less and less frequently. By now, over half of us had the bug and, weak and sickly as we were, wandering around so scantily dressed, standing half-naked in freezing conditions, we were constantly getting colds. The days passed and we lost track of one another, we'd lost our leader. Sometimes we'd see each other at a gay club and say hello in passing, as though the sisterhood was now in the past. Sometimes we shared our news, which didn't take long because our lives never changed. When we went to see Auntie Encarna she would nag us with gripes that sounded both reasonable and insane. She accused us of having abandoned her, said that we were living a suicidal existence, and complained that we couldn't see how difficult everything was for her. She called us opportunistic and ungrateful. "I gave you everything and this is how you repay me!" We'd missed Twinkle's first steps, his first words, we'd left her alone in a house that had once been ours too. The plants had completely taken over the patio, it was like being in the jungle or a chaotic greenhouse. Vines got tangled up in our high heels, bees buzzed brazenly in our faces, bats lurked among the creepers, and tree branches had blocked out the rectangle of sky. Auntie Encarna wandered this ungovernable kingdom with her increasingly obese son. He looked like a sumo wrestler. Fat and tyrannical, he hung off his mother's breasts, breasts that were now off-limits to johns.

Auntie Encarna had locked herself away in her house. The boy was all that mattered to her now. We'd lost our mother. Orphaned again. No one knew where to go, where to hide from what might happen.

BUT WHEN ONE OF US got sick, the others found out immediately. One night I heard that the injected silicon with which Lourdes molded her body had got into her bloodstream. Her AIDS-weakened body couldn't handle it. The silicon had given her breasts and rounded her thighs, plumped up her mouth and raised her cheekbones, but now it was running poisonously everywhere else, ravaging everything it touched. Suddenly, the thousand pesos she'd paid La Machi for her new body were her worst enemy. And so the whole travesti sisterhood mobilized. The music of our heels walking up the hospital steps, the tinkling of our jewelry, seemed, just for a moment, capable of redeeming the world. But La Machi met us with the news that there was nothing she could do. "The situation is irreversible. I am in so much pain, I have decided never to visit the regions of the gods again. I am not worthy of the privilege. Don't trust me, I have lied to you. I have given myself over to alcohol and endless sex, total promiscuity, I have blown this body up. But miracles exist, they're within reach. It's just hard to see them. Maybe that is our triumph: we're so innocent we can't see our own miracle."

After that the patient died a little more every day. Her mother stayed with her. She wasn't very outgoing. The patient smiled all the way through our visits. I never knew that a mother could say goodbye like that, from the dock, while her daughter drifted farther and farther out to sea until she was nothing but perfume. The drip marked the time. They kept saying there was hope until the very last. But they were lying, and in the minutes immediately after Lourdes's last breath we were completely undone, sobbing uncontrollably, curses flying from our tongues. Our mouths foamed like rabid dogs. We were tired of death.

THE MUSIC of our shoes played outside on the stairs, we left like we were fleeing a bombing raid. There was nothing we could say to one another. We couldn't speak of our sadness or our losses. We couldn't say a word. That night I went to the Park alone for the first time and for the first time was arrested by the police. They accused me of selling drugs. I spoke, I talked to them all night, about my friend's death, hunger, the bitterness of the travesti life, I groped them shamelessly, gave them all the money I had and left. Leaving everything behind. That is what it is to be a travesti. Did Lourdes think of herself as a boy at the end? At the very last, when the bug had won the war, was she ready to confront her childhood? To die you must be prepared to get your house in order, to acknowledge the boy you once were. To ask forgiveness for our many betrayals, for all the lies, the systematic deception, the errant path, for all the beauty we'd missed out on.

RIGHT FROM THE FIRST, she called me big-nose, ugly, a dark little mountain creature. She'd touched my dick shamelessly and made fun of how I talked: "Oh, she'll say hello like a fairy but her mouth is as dirty as a teamster's." Even though the pack accepted me immediately, she took her time before letting me into her life. She never said hello and the only time she ever spoke to me was to make fun of me. I'd go bright red in embarrassment and anger. I knew that it was better to laugh along but that didn't mean it didn't hurt. You needed a layer of blubber for the jokes not to get to you, not to want the earth to swallow you up. Her distinctive sense of humor was how she kept the pain at bay. She laughed at everything fiercely. She was never affectionate but she did have charm. She was like a chipped glass; you had to watch out for the sharp edges. A thousand times I saw her run for shelter with a face that shrank your soul, almost dragging herself along because of her limp. And a thousand times I saw her go back, she was incorrigible. She always picked pockets, always behaved badly, and was ready to drink ditch water, drugging herself with anything that she thought might enhance her wild adventures. She was brutal as only a lover can be. Being attacked by her was a delectable experience. "Big-nosed cocksucker! . . . Shitty little munchkin!" she'd spit before lighting a cigarette and looking around her with scorn, hating everything. She was cross-eyed and lame in one leg. Even so she maintained her beauty, it transcended her defects. In spite of the torrents of cheap alcohol that she poured into her body, she never fell over. But she got bitter when she drank, she lost track of her charm and became a malicious old lonely woman desperate to be touched, begging for love, for someone to reach out to her in the street, for one of us to leap over the barriers she put up and rescue her from the castle where she was hiding. "I don't know the words mother or father," she said to me one day. She looked away as she said it, adding drama to the moment so it would cut even deeper. She'd come down from Chaco on her own, when she was still a minor. She'd started out dressing as a woman only at night, she had a day job, did extra work on the side and on Friday and Saturday night arrayed herself in all the finery that poverty could provide: a bunch of two-peso rags tied together to form awful bras and miniskirts that looked as though they'd drop off or disintegrate at any moment. The struggle for beauty had worn us all down to the bone but we knew that if we stopped making an effort, we wouldn't survive out in the Park. Every day you had to cover your beard, wax your mustache, spend hours ironing your hair, walk in impossible shoes. There's no getting away from it: they were ridiculous, who on earth ever invented acrylic shoes so tall you could see the whole world from atop them, so tall that you never wanted to get off, so tall that johns asked you to please, keep them on, and licked them in the hope of tasting a little travesti glory, our profound frivolity, our big male feet in princess-whore shoes.

She walked on those heels better than anyone, with her beauty always on the edge of disappearing, snuffing out, abandoning her. Her name was Patricia but we called her the Cripple, the Ring, the Nut, or just Pato. "Patricia" was a tribute to a little sister she'd had in Chaco who died of fever alone at the farm. She'd only just found her body in time to save it from the pigs. She ran away from home that same day. She was fourteen and her parents hated her for being gay. She never asked permission: not to stay where she was or go wherever she wanted. She enjoyed taking on the name of her dead sister, she told me, on the same occasion she told me she didn't know the words mother or father. We were sitting on the sidewalk, waiting for the bus, it was a moment of rare intimacy. She made fun of me for my pussy voice, which is how people described it then, and I told her that people used to confuse me with my mother on the telephone.

She laughed and started rocking forward and back, unable to control herself. After a while she said, "I'd like to win the lottery and move somewhere. Go to live in Italy. I have a friend who lives like a queen out there. Here it's just problem after problem. You get into a car and gag on the smell of balls and ass. I just wish I could say to hell with it." And then it was like all of Mesopotamia had flooded into her eyes, all those swamps and folk songs, polkas playing on the desperately melancholy accordion she had inside of her. She turned away and said: "I don't know the words father and mother. I have no parents. I'm dead to them."

A car passed by, they called out to us and we got in with a pair of lovely specimens of the good life in Argentina. Two

well-fed lambs eager to have chunks bitten out of them. We
went to an apartment that belonged to one of them. Pato was
able to hide her limp by walking very slowly and exaggerat-
ing the waggle of her hips. She covered her squint with faded
pink glasses which were terribly fashionable at the time, and
which she never took off, not even in the shower. On the journey she'd continued teasing me for the way I talked, but cyn-
icism didn't suit me, I spoke that way naturally, so I let her
go on and on, laughing at her jokes because what else could
you do with a wild beast who played by her own rules, who
was only willing to learn up to a certain point, who rewarded
and punished herself according to her own criteria, like the
orphan she was, the poor orphan girl who was never taken to
the eye doctor, whose limp was never treated, who had stolen
the name of her dead sister.

The johns took us to an apartment on Calle Crisol. The
moment the security guard saw us, they chuckled maliciously
and exchanged jokes: "We've been caught with a couple of
guys," one of them said to the other. I was hurt but Pato knelt
down right there in the elevator, dug around in the crotch of
the more handsome one, and started to give him a blow job.
The other guy began to get nervous, I always got the timid
ones. He asked them to stop while his friend tried to take the
pink lenses off my friend and she said no, she'd had an eye
operation and needed them for protection. The idiot believed
her and when we got to the apartment we were in that moment of uncertainty when we weren't sure whether they were
going to be good to us or whether they were going to take advantage of our vulnerability. I wanted to leave. I thought they

were a couple of monumental idiots, one of them studied law, the other who knows what. But my friend tipped everything she had on her out onto the table, she was always loaded with substances that could get you high as a kite, and she offered it to the boys. One went nuts when he saw all that temptation on the table and the other, the timid one, told him to calm down, was it really worth it? But when things have got to a certain stage those kinds of questions don't have an answer.

Pato started rambling about how life was too cruel for a clear head and the timid one barked at her to shut up. If he'd only been polite to Pato that was as far as things would have gone. But there are millions of people in the world who don't deal with stress very well and my friend, in addition to fighting with me, got into it with her chongo's friend because she could never stand anyone telling her she couldn't do something, she took it as a big offense. The timid guy said that they weren't drug addicts and I got ready to leave, but Pato barked: "You're not going anywhere!" Then the two chongos started arguing. "It's all this faggot's fault!" said the law student, accidentally hitting Pato with his arm, an affront that set her off like a volcano. She leaped up and scratched him in the face before running off with her chongo's wallet.

The owner locked the apartment and told me not to move a muscle. I protested that it had nothing to do with me but they were angry about Pato scratching the law student's baby face. And that's when things turned really ugly, because I tried to leave but they grabbed me hard by the arm, sat me down, and began to get rough. They got a crazy look in their eyes, like they were capable of anything, which is when my whole body went tense. My hackles were raised: my lungs opened up, and I readied my nails to do as much damage as possible in case of attack. But they knew that I could make things difficult for them. I was holding all the trump cards, I could squeal like a pig, climb up the walls and knock over everything within reach, smash up all the cheap crockery they had in their student apartment, with those family photos that turn my stomach. I knew that if I really wanted to I could give them the battle they deserved, but then again fights like that were always exhausting so I backed down like a coward and used my words. I tried unconvincing arguments, saying I barely knew Pato, just from the Park, she wasn't really my friend, I didn't even know where she lived, like Peter betraying Jesus, but they didn't believe me. The law student was going nuts because Pato had taken his wallet with all his cards and ID, and the secret formula for Coca-Cola probably. I had the brilliant idea of suggesting that maybe she threw it away outside the moment she left, and he scurried out of there, leaving me alone with the timid one. I took advantage of the situation: I started to provoke him, purring in his ear, draping myself over him, raising my butt and waggling it until he started to give in some, then a little more and then we went into his room and I finished the job. He didn't just pay me, he walked me to the door where I sensed an opportunity to push things a little further, before it was completely over. I love that tantalizing moment of danger. I convinced him to come down with me in the elevator and we passed by the security guard, who said, "The gentleman is leaving already?" chortling to himself. When I saw their sly looks, which they didn't bother to hide, I shoved my john's hand right into my panties to keep the memory fresh and reveled in their embarrassment. As you know, a travesti is very hard to explain, everyone says so. Travestis are just as hard to explain to parents as they are to children.

I DIDN'T SEE PATO again until a long time after, one night when she sliced open another travesti's cheek for trying to steal a john from under her nose. The car had parked right on the border between their patches, Patricia saw the other woman open the door of the run-down Fiat Uno and lost her nut. She kicked the door closed, trapping the woman's fingers. When the car pulled away, it dragged the poor travesti along for a few feet while she screamed in anguish. I was there, with my little Coke bottle filled with rum, trying to earn a few more pesos so as to bring my night to an end, when the travesti managed to get her hand free and rolled over the asphalt. Then Pato pounced on her like a cougar and said, "I warned you to stop stealing my business," and cut open her cheek with a knife before running off down the hill into the Park. The few of us who were left took the injured party to the emergency room, where the on-call doctor asked, "So what do you girls have for us today?" Then he stitched up the wound himself and sent her home. "Be good," he called as we left.

We had no idea how to be good or bad, we wandered the world carrying the burden of our lives thus far, it fit in a purse bought on Calle San Martin or Ituzaingó. We did good and bad without a second's thought and occasionally we all met up for breakfast at McDonald's where people glared at us with the usual scorn. Sometimes we squabbled with each other like cats in a bag and ran off as a pack when we saw the patrol car belonging to the Guy from the Fourth Precinct, the famous Guy from the Fourth whom we were all so scared of.

On such occasions the best refuge is the ditch in the Park. In fact there are several. We lay down in them, which were of similar width and depth to coffins, like mummies, and covered ourselves with branches. We had marked out the hiding places, where you could no longer see the blue flashing lights of the patrol car. Sometimes the wait dragged on and we'd start to chat, lying in our sarcophagi. Thus I learned that Patricia had shacked up with a bum and they openly walked hand in hand in the street. I closed my eyes and pictured the scene as related to me by my friend lying in the ditch, her feet entangled in mine. Pato was waiting for the bus and the bum passed by asking for a few pesos. Feeling flirtatious, she gave them to him and he, to thank her, showed her the dead snake that dangled from his crotch all the way down to his knees. She reached out for it and weighed it up like an artisanal salami at a country fair. He told her to be careful, she could get hurt, and she replied that nothing could hurt her anymore, what she had in her hands least of all. And so they walked off from the bus stop together, bought a beer along the way, and ended up in Plaza Austria, a favorite spot for orgies involving rapacious, perfumed homosexuals hunting for the corpse of love, a land of the toothless and marginalized, the broken and unhinged, the dead and the gutted. But she wasn't afraid of anything and he was like a puppy abandoned in the middle of the night. And so they consummated their union in the middle of no-man's-land.

Pato took him home with her and started to support him. They lived in her little cinder block house on Coronel Olmedo with its unfinished cracked cement floor, which was cold as a winter's morning. She pressed the bum without a past, with no mother or father, no place to go, no ambition or courage, against her, and took him for herself. One night he came with her to the Park. They'd just come from the municipal stadium where they'd spent their time picking the pockets of the crowd. She called him "my husband" in front of anyone who cared to listen and almost started something with another travesti because she thought she was looking at him, but he was rather too old and malnourished to catch anyone's eye so it blew over quickly. Just the same, I chose not to look at him too hard. They reminded me of a disabled couple I once saw at the pharmacy, her body had been twisted into a kind of X, one leg pointed one way, the other the opposite, and he was a little slow-witted and foamed a touch at the edge of his mouth as he handed over his prescription, doing his best to communicate with the pharmacist. Afterward I followed them downtown, a few steps behind, thinking that sometimes everything really does seem right with the world when even the sick and the lame can find love.

It can all be so beautiful, so fertile, so unexpected that it's hard to believe it was all the work of one god alone. Language is mine. It is my right, a part of it belongs to me. It came to me, I didn't go looking for it, so it is truly mine. I inherited it from my mother, my father squandered it. I'm going to wreck it, to make it sick, to confuse it, unsettle it, tear it apart and bring it back to life as often as seems necessary, a new dawn for every well-made thing in this world.

A FEW WEEKS LATER it was Twinkle in Her Eye's third birthday. I gave him a little music box that played "Autumn Leaves" when you turned a handle. Like a model pianola. I thought that music would sit well in Twinkle's palms and it seemed a nice gift. Auntie Encarna looked tired. She said that it was easier to raise a child as a father. She said that fathers don't form such close emotional bonds with their children. But she was tied to Twinkle, her destiny was entwined with his. If they were ever separated, she wouldn't be able to go on living. Meanwhile, Maria the Bird looked up at us with her pomegranate eyes, pecking at the crumbs on the tablecloth.

CALLE 27 DE ABRIL, at two in the morning. I strutted down Sobremonte Alley, the street was deserted. I was wearing blue tights that I'd stolen from my mother, a short vest, and a small backpack that barely had space for my house keys, condoms, and lust for money. Single men stared at me, and the couples whispered to each other. They were shameless, they didn't care that I could see them inspecting me like I was on sale. Their indiscretion was perfectly respectable, but the way I dressed was a violation. I was all they could look at. Such is the power of travestis, we attract the gazes of the world. No one can escape the allure of a man dressed as a woman, the faggots who go too far, the degenerates everyone stares at.

Insomnia made me daring: I set myself impossible targets, like not going to bed until I'd earned enough money to pay the month's rent or for a wig or one of the other absurd things for which I was willing to sacrifice what I'd earned with the sweat of my body, the body of a disgraced travesti. Of course, I rarely achieved my objective and went to bed without having managed to meet a single fucking target. The taste of frustration was one of the main causes of my insomnia. There's little worse than going to bed with your eyes wide open, with the taste of poverty in your mouth.

Sometimes I miscalculated during the negotiation, asking too much of miserly or poverty-stricken men, or at least men who weren't remotely willing to pay what my intuition suggested they should. Other times it was a question of taste: I couldn't stand the idea of sleeping with certain especially repulsive specimens. That was my sacred rule: not to get into the car of anyone I found repugnant.

But I wasn't having much luck that Tuesday night. I was walking home down 27 de Abril when I heard a car slow down, lured by the sway of my hips. I looked all around, there didn't seem to be any unwanted witnesses in sight. The tinted window of the driver's seat came down to reveal a bald skull followed by a pair of thick, hairy eyebrows, a mustache, and a voice saying, "How are you doing, gorgeous?"

I recognized the voice and the timbre. I knew that I'd heard it before, it was someone who was once very famous. I couldn't remember his name. But it was him.

I traveled back in time, to when I was seven or eight and we were spending Christmas and New Year's at my grandma's house in the Los Bulevares neighborhood. I saw my girl cousins, recent entries into adolescence, their chests bulging a little with the udders they'd grown since last Christmas, lit up with lust for boys and drenched in suffocating quantities of perfume. I saw my boy cousins dancing and their girlfriends watching out to see whom they looked at, desperately jealous of hussies trying to steal their catch. I saw my grandparents sitting in a pair of chairs in the garden, watching their offspring dance with stupid smiles on their faces.

Suddenly I remembered who this john propositioning me on 27 de Abril was: the folk singer who so delighted my family during my childhood, whose music rang out from every house in the neighborhood. My girl cousins sang along with a hand on their hearts, like it was the national anthem. Even though years had passed and he was old and bald, and an aura of failure had settled around his magnificent truck, I decided to get in to pay homage to all the memories thumping around to the beat of his music in my chest. I took him back to my room, apologizing for its poverty, the small bed, the sparse furniture (what there was clashed), and the tacky knickknacks hanging from the walls. He was surprised to see that I'd kept my toys from childhood. He wore cheap cologne, the kind my father wore on his alcoholic pilgrimages to the bars in town. All his friends used the same aftershave, which was worse than dog's breath: a viscous vulgarity that stank up the air. I may have been poor, but I smelled of Calvin Klein. I knew the huge difference between not wearing anything and putting on that nasty stuff. The chasm of pretension. My singer got undressed, life on tour had transformed his body into one more befitting a pregnant street cur. I did my thing as best I could, with the little love I was able to summon up on that exhausting night. But he seemed to like it, saying, "Little girl, this way," "Little girl, get up here," "Little girl, don't do that."

Just when we finally got into sync, someone knocked on the window. At that, he got anxious, very anxious. He scrambled for his clothes, saying that he was a public figure, he thought we'd be left alone, I'd lied to him. As we argued, the other john got bored of knocking. It was my only chance to thank this idol from the past for the nights of happiness and dance in my childhood, but I couldn't get him to relax. I tried a thousand tricks to have him forgive me, I swore that it had never happened before, which was true: I'd never been interrupted by another john while riding a famous folk singer.

But it was no use. And to top it all, he refused to pay me. He left in a huff, his four-by-four screeching off down the deserted street. Before leaving, he had me make sure that the coast was clear, to protect his battered image. I was left shaking with frustration and pleasure in a room that now stank of his sleazy aftershave. I just wanted to get to a phone and call my cousins to remind them of those Christmases when they kissed under the fig tree and danced like crazy to that man's songs, when life seemed like a cactus flower blossoming out of tough skin.

Once the sound of his enormous truck had disappeared into the distance, I made myself some tea and sat down to write, something I often did after my rounds. But I didn't manage a page. The other john came back when he saw that the truck was gone, knocked on my window, and I had no choice but to stop writing and get back to work.

HUNTING SEASON was officially open. We started to be harassed by the entire neighborhood. They were thirsty for travesti blood. It was in the newspapers, made the TV news, and would later be documented in history books: "Today we commemorate the slaughter of the travestis."

Twinkle wasn't safe at Auntie Encarna's house. The graffiti had got worse, as did the insults, which were getting more and more pointed. We wore disguises on the street: scarves, hats, caps, shawls, our hearts in our mouths as we waited for someone to come to the door. Where were my parents at the time? How can this life be possible?

ONE NIGHT I got into a car with two very friendly guys with brown hair who took me to a corner store in Barrio Yofre, by the railway tracks. It was three in the morning. On the way, the one driving said he liked my perfume. They offered me cocaine from a baggy that someone had torn open with their teeth. I was in the back with one of them, doing my thing. Not the cramped quarters in a small car nor the passing traffic can stop me from doing my thing. I liked them both, especially the one next to me. The driver parked the car in the middle of that bleak part of town and we went into the store in silence. It was run by the driver's mother and she was a light sleeper. In the storage room at the back, a kind of purgatory zone between the store and the house, between bags of candy and crates of beer, I got to work. Suddenly the owner's son told us to be quiet. We could hear his mother calling for him, asking who was there and what they were doing. "Nothing, Ma, we came to pick up some beer. Go back to sleep, it's late," he called. But his mother went on and on and eventually the guy told us we had to go somewhere else.

The other one, the one I liked, suggested his apartment a few blocks away. We got dressed, broke camp after taking a few bottles of beer from the refrigerator, and went on to the next place. This time, the guy I liked drove. He was like a gift from heaven. There wasn't an ounce of skin on him that I wasn't tempted by. He smelled good, dressed well, had green eyes and a chiseled body. His companion was different: an edgy, scrawny cocaine addict who smelled bad, dressed worse, and was clumsy with me.

We arrived. It was almost four in the morning. The street was deserted. We went inside and they asked me to lie on the bed. That's when your survival instincts kick in: my feelers went out like a snake tasting the air. It's when the john starts acting naturally, when they feel they have a right to demand things. All prostitutes get goose bumps about then. Prostitutes should only do what they're comfortable with: the john's wishes are immaterial. A whore with any sense of self-worth never gives in. This is when the john needs to bend to the wishes of the whore, believing that it's what they wanted all along. And they need to pay for it. There was a large jar on the nightstand, the kind they use to keep olives in, but this was full of coins. The walls were decorated with martial-arts-style weaponry. Different-sized sticks, as phallic as you like. The boys gave me cocaine and ecstasy. The apartment was horrible. The place was deathly ugly, it reminded me of my parents' decor.

I was naked in bed. They got undressed too and started to play with me. All three bodies were naked but one was appreciably more vulnerable than the other two. Letting yourself go in these situations makes you dizzy. I began to feel light-headed and nauseated. I asked them to give me some time to catch my breath and they moved off. Then I just tamely fell asleep. I'd never slept like that in my life. Everything simply froze and went black. When I opened my eyes again it was dawn. Harsh light streamed in through the curtains. They were dressed now, sitting at the computer, watching porn and drinking beer. At first I couldn't remember where I was or with whom. The monitor was playing images of naked girls, all of whom were asleep while being penetrated by the sticks hanging on the walls, with bottles, with their own arms. Suddenly I saw myself on screen with a bottle of beer coming out of my ass and one of their faces resting on my butt cheek. A lovely image for the Christmas card. I pretended to still be asleep. I couldn't hear what they were saying. I felt very weak. Then I passed out again. I dreamed of a riverbank, a lovely town on the prettiest river in the world. It was sunset, I was walking down the bank into the water, willow trees blocked out the sky. I wanted to go back to the town, back to my room. Bats the size of humans hung from the branches. They were asleep. On the ground, spread out like leftovers from a feast, were the massive bones of cows, with flies and pools of blood. I woke up feeling disgusted.

I managed to lift myself up on my arms, touched myself, and immediately knew that they'd done what they liked with me. The sheets were stained with semen, shit, and blood. They still had their backs to me, looking at the computer. I cleared my throat. "You fell asleep," they said. Really. My eyelids felt heavy. It was cold. The sun wasn't streaming in anymore but the light hurt just the same. I went back to sleep.

When I woke up I saw the one I liked lying next to me, he'd fallen asleep too. The other one, the unpleasant one, was still taking cocaine at the computer. He was jerking off naked. When he saw that I was awake he came over and wanted another round but couldn't keep his erection. Instead of giving up, he kept on trying. His friend woke up and started to watch. The impotent one got angry with me, telling me I couldn't keep his dick hard. I didn't have the strength, but far from giving up, I acted. I acted better than Jessica Lange, Anna Magnani, Annie Girardot, and Marlene Dietrich put together, I summoned all my acting goddesses and they came to my aid. I pretended to be attracted to my aggressor. The other one was a little more sober. He'd woken up in a good mood, the piece of shit. I pulled him over and told him I wanted to finish the party with him alone. I wasn't going to charge but said we should go to my house so we could get some peace and quiet. At home I had every pleasure he could think of. I was a girl armed to the teeth with party supplies.

He brought a note of sanity to the proceedings. He called a taxi for his friend and took me home in his car. On the way I started to shake. I thought that I was going to die then and there. "Don't you die in my car, honey," he said. I could barely answer.

When we got to the boardinghouse, I collapsed against the door trying to get my key in the lock. He got scared. He dragged me inside and disappeared. I slept the whole day through. When I woke up I checked the time, day, and month. Then I took a bath as quick as I could and rushed out to college. A professor was waiting for me.

BEREFT OF ANGIE and Auntie Encarna, the Park had been losing its allure for a while but it was ruined entirely when they flooded it with light. It was decided that the underground world in which we plied our trade, the beautiful shadows, needed to come to an end. We aren't creatures of light, we're beasts of the dark, furtive in our movements, which are practically frictionless, like our resistance. Light exposes us, it drives us away. We couldn't live with the new life that had begun to populate the Park.

And so the exodus of the travestis began. We left, driven out of paradise, like refugees from a bombing campaign. We saw the city differently from other people, we had to find another promised land where we could work our charms once more. The Park was given over to athletes, families, art schools, and a new police station that claimed to be fighting the war against drugs with their vans and sirens.

Off go the travestis on their high heels, rotten legs for useless tables. Dragging themselves along, away from the dark land of dappled green beauty.

Deprived of our refuge, harassed by the light, we decided to rethink our business, reassessing our corners, choosing to work from our apartments and to take advantage of every opportunity that came along. Again, we were banished into solitude, our ties cut off. We couldn't reach one another. Our bond was based on seeing each other regularly, but without a place to gather it grew weak. Society wouldn't countenance us being all together so it had driven us from the Park. We had always been in death's antechamber, on the shores of Lethe, but now we were being forced to try the waters.

I CHOSE THE BALCONY of my room as my new place of work. A low little balcony that framed my travesti outlook. I had to wait until very late to use it. I couldn't be seen by my roommates or the owner. And I had to disguise the reason why I was standing on the balcony like a false virgin usurping the traditional maiden's role.

And so I became a witness to the nightlife of the neighborhood. I saw rats the size of a cat, dogfights, domestic quarrels, heard the neighbors' moans during sex in the middle of the night. I was a silent, invisible witness to muggings and beatings, the girls running down the street in tears, the parades of partygoers returning home in every state imaginable. A lonely world that offered a rare and pleasant opportunity for contemplation.

I knew how to live like that, without seeing my sisters. Our paths didn't cross anymore. My visits to see Auntie Encarna grew more and more seldom. I was ready to live that way. I can be alone. They had taught me to survive.

ONE DAY, I decided to go visit her, but there was no answer at the door. I waited, aware of the inquiring glances of neighbors who were always ready with a mocking or offensive remark. The week before, Abigail had been hit by a stone as she came back with the weekly groceries. I saw a man walking down the street holding the hand of a boy dressed in checked kindergarten overalls. I stared at them enthralled, high on marijuana and my disguise. They were beautiful. Once they'd reached me, the man whispered in my ear, "You gave me a fright, I almost passed right by." I didn't react, so he added, "It's me, Encarna."

I stared at them in surprise and suddenly recognized our mother under a face fuzzed up by a beard and baggy clothes that didn't quite conceal her breasts. Twinkle had grown up at the speed of light, he could already say my name. Encarna let me in after the boy and slammed the door shut behind her. We went into the jungly heart of her patio.

"Everything changes," said Auntie.

Maria the Bird had been locked in a cage strategically positioned to protect her from the cats.

"She doesn't sing anymore," said Auntie Encarna as she removed her male disguise and made a snack for her son.

Yes, things change but not so much. Underneath, indomitable, appeared the body of the woman I missed like crazy, the body of our mother whom we'd renounced without knowing why. Auntie Encarna pointed to Maria and told me that it was Twinkle who noticed the cats hunting her. He had started screaming and pointing: "Auntie! Auntie!" Poor Maria didn't know how to take care of herself. She never had.

Twinkle took her out of her cage and she started to peck at breadcrumbs on the table. I didn't know what to say. Encarna said that she dressed like that to take him to kindergarten, so people wouldn't start asking questions. The mother of one his school friends wanted to invite Twinkle over, she said the boys got on well, but Encarna wasn't sure. She'd got Twinkle his documentation.

"He's my son, no one can take him away from me now."

Maria ate breadcrumbs. Occasionally she looked at me but her eyes were devoid of personality. Encarna said that it was out of fear: after she was attacked by the cats she lost her humanity and stopped flying. Encarna's voice was heavy with sadness. Then she turned on the TV and put Twinkle in Her Eye in front of a children's show. She took an exercise book out of his backpack and showed me Twinkle's drawings, in crayon, in every color. He'd drawn her as a man and a woman with him in the middle holding both their hands. He'd drawn himself firing golden rays from his heart like the sun.

With a chipped, unpainted nail and a bare finger denuded of rings, Auntie Encarna pointed to the two versions and told me that she'd told the kindergarten that she was a widower.

"I said that his mother died during labor. I did it for him, so he can live a normal life. His ID card says that his name is Antonio Ruiz. It's also why I grew my beard, for the ID photo."

Auntie Encarna had gone respectable. She was living the life of a chameleon, adapting to the world as it is. She said that Twinkle knew everything. We didn't need to hide anything from him. The boy was very smart. Just then he looked up from the TV and said, "Yes, I know everything. She's my mommy and my daddy. Not many children are so lucky."

I thought about how the love in every family eventually breaks down. But they weren't a family. The word was too insignificant for what they were. Their love was much greater, it was all the empathy of which humans are capable.

"He never makes a mistake," said Auntie. "Out there he always calls me Daddy and in here I'm Mommy. It would be hard if he weren't so smart."

Maria the Bird jumped off the table, trying to fly, but she fell to the ground. Twinkle picked her up and cupped his hands around her. Then he began to whisper to her, trying to put her to sleep. Maria succumbed and went still. Twinkle got up and went to his room.

"Not a word," said Encarna.

I did exactly as she said. I didn't say a word and we sat in silence, drinking maté as night fell in the patio.

THE NEWS REACHED ME, brought by carrier pigeons passing in the night: Natali had died. She was found in the back room after locking herself in on the night of the full moon. Sandra, who was staying at Auntie Encarna's, hiding from dealers who accused her of paying them with false bills, found her. She'd come out to the patio to look at the frost: it was the day it almost snowed in the city. It was so cold and quiet she knew immediately that death was abroad in the house. She called Auntie Encarna and no one answered. Then she called the other girls but didn't get an answer from them either. Eventually she went to the room where Natali had locked herself in and found the lock broken and our friend lying on the floor like a dead dog, frozen and heavy as a chest full of books. Sandra embraced the deceased body until the cold threatened to take her too. Then she went to look for a blanket; she may have been past warming up, but our she-wolf, the only travesti who hated the full moon, deserved a measure of dignity. She cried until the rest of us arrived, which we did in dribs and drabs, led by Auntie Encarna and Twinkle, as word reached us.

In the blind alley where all travesti lives end up, we were always battling against the elements, trying to swap a dead body for a living one, a body that breathes and holds out, that can withstand the thousand deaths with which the fates have strewn our path. And so Sandra mourned Natali while a part of her still clung to the naive hope that the she-wolf might still wake up the way she did after all her lock-ins. Not this time.

One by one we tried to console Sandra and mourn our sister. Auntie Encarna greeted us with recriminations about how we'd stopped visiting her since the neighborhood had turned hostile, calling us cowards.

"The only reason I don't throw you out is because I don't want my son believing that his mother repays shit with more shit. I want him to learn to repay shit with flowers, I want him to know that flowers grow out of shit. So I'm not turning you away: I understand the pain of the dead dog, here among us, the wandering bum we considered a friend. My son won't learn about the miseries of the world from his mother. There's a dead dog in my patio. She was our sister. We're all of the same stock and we're all going to die one day, just like her. The funeral is out back, come on through."

Our medicine woman, La Machi, was already there. She'd returned to magic after Lourdes's death, smoking her cigar and gargling with wine as she ran her hand over Natali's dead body. Our voices united in a sad, black, cyclical, unending song. We sang in warbling voices straining to reach the high notes but also strained by the ritual, it was as though we knew it would be the last rite we would share: our time of covens, exchanging wigs and dresses, secrets and tears, songs and benders, was coming to an end on that frozen morning. The foundations on which our history had been built were crumbling, the columns of our magic, our religion, were inexorably giving way.

Little by little our extended family, the good johns, began to
arrive. Well-built, sexy Black men carrying with them their
burden of slavery. Men from the Far East with their ancestral
understanding of sorrow. The Headless Men queued up on the
sidewalk and let everybody come in before them, hats in hand,
with the knowing gazes of those who have seen a thousand
wars. Even our most venerable colleagues, the mothers of all
travestis, whom we'd assumed had passed on long ago, made
an appearance with their weathered rags and faces etched with
wrinkles. Their souls too had been touched by the death of the
only travesti she-wolf, born a seventh son, godchild to a president of the republic.

Travesti heaven must be as beautiful as the stunning
landscapes of our memory, somewhere to spend eternity
without getting bored. Travesti she-wolves who die in winter
are welcomed with special pomp and joy, into another world
where they receive all the goodness denied to them in this.

Meanwhile, those of us who are left behind embroider
our death shrouds with sequins.

AFTER THE WAKE, I left the Park for good. I didn't
want anything to do with anyone. I chose not to know, I exer-
cised my right to keep sadness at bay. I had watched so many
die already. I didn't want to see anyone else go. The whores
who had been my friends had disappeared. We sent each
other smoke signals, flares, underground messages occasionally but the harassment by the police never let up.

I'll never really know who left whom: if it was us, when we split up, when we let them into our territory, who brought sadness to the Park by abandoning it, or it was the other way around. Trade had started to drop off, there were fewer and fewer johns, they were just as afraid as we were of getting caught in the act by the police. The newspapers and television said that the new lighting in the Park would bring an end to crime and prostitution. I always thought they regarded us as cockroaches: they just had to turn on the light to send us all scuttling away.

But when we lost the Park we lost a support network that came just from being there all together. We could defend each other in case of attack, share johns when we had too much on our plate, fix each other's makeup, share a hip flask of gin, or just chat when the cold and desolation got really bad. Several stayed in touch with me because I was the youngest of the pack and they all wanted to act as my fairy godmother. Some gave me good advice, others gave the best advice they could.

LITTLE BY LITTLE I started to work in the streets around my neighborhood. Some of the taxi drivers and johns already knew me as the Girl on Calle Mendoza. My boarding-house was right in the middle of the block. The night of the Man with the Black Umbrella it was raining. It was three in the morning. I'd spent over a week eating nothing but brown bread and tea, but I didn't want to go to work. Through the sickly drizzle that had driven away all the passersby, I saw from my balcony a figure in an overcoat walking casually along. He was dressed all in black with a black umbrella that must have been expensive because even from my window you could see the gleam of the wooden handle. I think it was the nicest umbrella I've ever seen in my life.

As he came closer, I realized that he was drunk, but that didn't matter. I'd never had any problem with that: alcoholism was frequent among my johns and I had been hardened by my father's habit. Some of us refused to work with drunks, they couldn't stand the violence alcohol brought out in men. And then there were the ones who couldn't get it up or took ages to come. But the Man with the Black Umbrella was so handsome that I didn't care he was drunk. When you're tired of giving love to the ugly, coming across a john with an ivory smile, who tells you how pretty you are in the rain while you're standing up on your balcony, and who has the good sense not to mention Romeo or Juliet, is a genuine stroke of luck.

The price of love was thirty pesos with no time limit. The Man with the Black Umbrella thought that was fair, so he came in and got undressed. He was pale and skinny. A very polite albino lizard. Mostly, drunks act like clowns, making a huge effort to seem gallant, but he didn't. We did what we could with the materials we had to work with and then I gave him permission to spend the night.

It's never a good idea to sleep with a client. Plenty of us have woken up the next day to find our homes ransacked. Others weren't so lucky: their bodies barely made the news, little more than roadkill. But I was tired and fell asleep next to him in the bed I'd had since I was ten, which hurt me like a bitten tongue when I had to use it professionally.

I was woken by the noise. The drunk was vomiting to one side of the bed, all over my dress and shoes. I stood up and tried to rub his back, to help or comfort him, but he pushed me away and went on vomiting. Between gags he mumbled *I'm sorry, so sorry, so sorry*, but he was so drunk that he could barely speak. When he was done, he straightened up a little, pulled down his boxers and started to piss against the wall. Either he didn't notice or he didn't care that he was splashing the bed too. He just murmured, bright red with embarrassment, *I'm sorry, so sorry, so sorry.*

When he was done, he started trying to clean up, but I told him he'd better just leave, just pay me and leave. He dug into the pockets of his pants, which were hanging from the back of a chair, took out his wallet, threw thirty pesos on the table, and started to get dressed. I've always enjoyed the way drunks get dressed, the lack of logic, the odd moment of balance. When he'd finally buttoned up his shirt he dug back into his pants, while I watched, crouched naked in one corner of the bed, trying not to think about my vomit-covered dress and shoes. Suddenly he said, "I'm missing a hundred pesos."

I told him he must have lost them on the way, he'd been very drunk the night before. But he insisted that I'd taken a hundred pesos from him. He grabbed the three tens he'd left on the table and put them in his pocket.

"Nobody steals a hundred pesos from me," he said as he did up his fly with clumsy drunken hands, fumbling through vomit. Eventually he gave up on it, took a knife from his pocket, flicked it smoothly open, and pointed it at my throat: "Give me my hundred pesos."

He threw me down on the bed, choking me with one hand while the other pressed the blade against my skin, telling me to give him back his hundred pesos. Even though I was barely able to breathe I told him he could search the house if he liked but he wouldn't find them. He let me go to do just that, but as he stood up he stepped in a puddle of his own vomit, slipped and fell on all fours.

Maybe he saw himself at that moment, splashing around in his own vomit and piss, threatening a twenty-year-old travesti with a switchblade over a hundred pesos he must have spent on booze hours before. Then he returned to his previous litany: *I'm so sorry, so sorry, so sorry,* while I reached for a gun I kept under the bed to defend myself in just that kind of situation and told him to leave the thirty pesos he owed me and go. He left his whole wallet. He didn't even bother to take out the bills. He grabbed his black overcoat and left with tears in his eyes. I heard him continuing to murmur his chant down the hall and waited until I couldn't hear him anymore before getting up and making a start on cleaning up the mess.

Only when the door out to the street had closed did I realize that he'd forgotten his umbrella with the lovely handle. I used it for years, until I lost it somewhere, I don't know how. People always admired it, saying how distinguished and valuable it must be, and I agreed. In fact, it was what I said to myself as I scrubbed the floor and wall and changed the sheets, dried out the mattress, washed my dress and rubbed my shoes with cotton wool soaked in alcohol.

When I woke up after midday, I invited some friends to tea paid for with the thirty pesos and they all agreed that it was a good way to spend the money, taking turns to admire my new umbrella.

I MADE AN APPOINTMENT with La Machi and went to her apartment, which was in a complex, at the end of a long, damp corridor that didn't exactly evoke spiritual enlightenment. She was waiting in the threshold, smoking one of her cigars, wearing a robe and flip-flops. Through the door wafted a pair of black cats as if they were being exhaled. They ran through my legs and disappeared.

"Don't worry," she said. "They're females, they'll be fine."

She showed me into the apartment, which was full of carpets and crochet rugs. A porn film was playing on the TV. She took the towel from her head and dried her hair in front of me sitting with her legs open and head bowed.

"What brings you here?"

I started to talk, not really knowing what I was saying, and suddenly I burst into tears. She didn't look at me. Her hair was all she seemed to care about. I told her that I was tired. I had come out of exhaustion. My hair had been falling out for a while now. One night especially was awful: I started to shed locks of hair onto a john's body, like snowflakes. When he got up from bed, his silhouette was there on the sheets, drawn in my hair.

"I don't want to go bald," I sobbed.

La Machi told me that I didn't need any medicine. She still had her head between her legs, now she was brushing her long red hair, which fell right down to the ground. From there, without looking at me, she said that the male body is always trying to reassert itself. It never leaves us be, it resents what we do to it. I asked what that was.

"You don't know yet?"

After a while she added that there were treatments, hormones that stimulated hair growth. And that I wasn't to get upset, it could be much worse. When she was done with her hair she went to the kitchen and came back with a tray of cookies and two cups of coffee.

"The problem is you have a sad, dark little gnome inside of you," she said.

I had to watch out for the gnome. I wasn't sad or dark: it was the gnome who was sometimes dormant and sometimes woke up and wanted to take over. The cats slipped in through the window and lay down next to each other on the orange leatherette sofa.

"They lose their hair too. Lots of it. I don't know what to do with it all," said La Machi, stroking them. The cats let her. They looked like they could easily spend the day there without deigning to look at us once. "I think their attitude to sleep is very wise," said La Machi. "Sometimes it's all a matter of sleep."

I left without telling her my deepest fear: that the more my hair fell out, the more I would look like my father. I knew that it was tiredness, that it was all a matter of getting some rest. But my forehead got broader and broader and the male face lurking under it grew more and more threatening.

PEOPLE CAME UP with several explanations for San-dra's suicide. For example, some said dealers from Bella Vista were still looking for her over the forged banknotes. But one of the dealers was Sandra's boyfriend. A guy they called Pacú, because he was from Entre Rios like the fish, and also be-cause his dick was the size of a pacú. It was so big it looked a little deformed. But that wasn't enough to make Sandra happy. Even though her bodily needs were seen to by the beast, Sandra always wandered around with a long face and sad old puppy eyes.

She got worse after she found Natali's body. It was a dif-ficult period for us: it seemed like every day we got news that another member of the pack had died. But Sandra had been insecure since birth: she had trouble dealing with misfor-tune. For her, the least setback was the end of the world. Then she met a chew toy who made all her decisions for her, he han-dled the money and decided when she'd work. Sandra started selling some stuff on her boyfriend's behalf because he was a typical capitalist bastard who forced her to do his dirty work. He was cowardly, cheap, cunning, and grabby. But give credit where credit is due: he also made chocolate-covered pancakes with dulce de leche in about two minutes and they were always perfect, it was the only manifestation of beauty of which he was capable. But there's no doubt that Pacú got her more and more involved in drug dealing, Sandra and other unwary girls like her, and soon the red-light district was full of young women selling what they didn't have just to keep him happy. Sandra had got a little tired of it and started to work reluctantly, slipping him a few false bills. As punishment, Pacú had kicked her in the solar plexus until a few of us who happened to be around intervened.

But it wasn't true, like some people said, that Sandra had killed herself because of Pacú and his partners. And neither was it true that it was a psychotic breakdown. She'd certainly had breakdowns, like that time she started wandering around Plaza España half-naked and screaming, between cars whose drivers honked their horns and shouted insults at her while she screeched "Crazy like your mother!" in their faces with her breasts hanging out. We had to wait for the lights to turn red before coming to her rescue. That time she scratched, kicked, and bit us until we'd managed to get her onto the sidewalk and rearranged her clothes. We tried to calm her down, but it was useless. We ended up at the psychiatric hospital, where she made herself its most popular patient every time she was admitted.

Because of her history, it was easy just to say that Sandra had gone mad again. But those of us more familiar with suicide knew immediately, because of the discreet way in which she chose to return death's embrace, that it was on account of sheer sadness. To put an end to the suffering, she had downed a bunch of colorful pills and lain down in bed perfectly made up with her hair done wearing a modest spring dress from another age. She left water and food for her dog Coco and the door ajar for when they ran out and she found herself without a mistress. Sandra also hoped that the half-open door would ensure she'd be found in pristine condition. But, as usual, she was out of luck: when she was discovered, her body was bloated, pale, and stinking. There was no letter of farewell, but there was a note stuck to the refrigerator with a magnet saying that all her furniture was to go to Auntie Nené, who had finally dared to come out as a travesti at an advanced age and didn't even have anywhere to drop dead.

And so that was the unfortunate end of our sister Sandra: a nut, suicide, and petty drug dealer, always indecisive, the biggest whore of us all, who always stained her skin with hair wax and never said goodbye, who was raped in prison and supplied us with Rohypnol, who boasted about having once serviced a governor. Sweet, sad Sandra.

AFTER HER SUICIDE, we tried to look after each other better. We avoided making hurtful jokes and even indulged in a hug or two.

I went looking for other nests. I asked for help. But some of my sisters knew no other life. It had always been their world since the world began, it was their only reality. If you don't believe me, look at that pair of ugly travestis who cross the street when someone calls out an insult from inside a garage. The older uses the stone in her ring to scratch each of the cars on the block lined up waiting for their turn with the mechanic.

I DON'T KNOW precisely in what order the threats came. Apparently the father of one of Twinkle's kindergarten friends had once been one of Auntie Encarna's johns and knew her secret. Envelopes were slipped under the front door, more graffiti appeared on the house's facade, anonymous phone calls were made. Each new threat wore down Encarna's patience a little more. a day came when she decided it was pointless to paint over the scrawls and instead let them accumulate so that the inevitable spelling errors were superimposed.

The Crow sisters were also suspects, the little rich girls were well capable of doing something so nefarious. One day we visited Auntie Encarna and found her deeply distraught. She met us bathed in tears. Twinkle, locked in his room, was crying too. We asked what happened and she said that she'd hit her son. He'd infuriated her so that she'd hit him and now she wanted to die, she wished her hands would turn to stone. She was beside herself, it was hard to take in. I decided to go to the boy's room, knocked on his door, and the hefty tremor of his clairvoyance made me shiver. The room exuded the anguish of someone who can see the future but doesn't know what to do about it.

Twinkle was hiding under the sheets. He told me to go away, but just before I left him alone he said: "It won't come. You might think that it'll come one day, but no. It never will." When I looked at him I knew what he was talking about. I knew that this child had just said something I never wanted to hear, not even from myself. I wondered, and wanted to ask, why he had said it to me, but the boy had gone back to being the scared little child who'd just been hit by the person he loved most in the world. The oracle had closed himself off, gone away. I went over, hugged him, and tried to console him. It was the purest act of maternity, something shared by all the females of the world, hugging a defenseless creature, giving them affection, calming their terror. Auntie Encarna was howling through the door for him to forgive her. Even though we couldn't see her, we knew that she was on her knees, her face streaked with mascara and tears, cracked hands at her chest, the gremlin of sorrow holding her feet to the fire. I opened the door. Twinkle said that he'd forgive her if only she'd stop shouting.

When I left the house a little while later I thought to myself that I couldn't do what Auntie Encarna did: give all of myself. Sacrifice everything for someone. I didn't understand what kind of love that was, all I knew was that I wasn't capable of it. Which meant that I didn't deserve to receive it either. The boy was right: love wouldn't come because it knew that I couldn't accept it with good grace.

The night was humid, coating every nook and cranny with its blue shadow. Not even those oh-so-eighties lamps on Calle Alberdi had any effect. At the corner of Paso de los Andes and 27 de Abril was a funeral home whose doors were always open. A car slowed down to match my speed and the driver asked me how I was doing. I never answer that question honestly: generally I reply with a number and start haggling, like I'm in a Persian bazaar. Men don't just withhold their affection, they're also stingy about the money they spend on pleasure. However, to my surprise, this time I answered, "Things have been better, I've been better, but I can't complain."

"Can I give you a lift somewhere?" he asked then, and something about the way he said it made me stop dead in my tracks. The mourners who'd stepped out of the funeral home for a cigarette looked over at us and I felt a little embarrassed. I looked harder and saw that he was very handsome, really very handsome, his eyes were as bright as his tone, he was graying like Richard Gere and he opened his door with a smile. He knew that that was his purpose in the world, to smile, to use the mouth that God gave him. He wasn't desperate or in a hurry, he didn't try to grope me the moment I sat next to him. He spoke to me as though I was someone special, a dear friend or a first date, which was unusual. He told me that it was his last night in Córdoba, he was staying at the NH hotel on Cañada, that it had a lovely view, and asked if I'd like to go with him. I said that I would, so long as he agreed to my price. He smiled: "No need to be rude."

We quickly agreed on a fee and he asked me whether I liked music. I said that I did, a lot, but not what he was listening to. I told him about a station that always plays jazz around that time. He asked me to turn to it and soon Lester Young's saxophone was bathing us with its sadness. A couple of blocks farther on he asked if I minded him smoking in the car. I said that I did and he apologized and put away the cigarette he was about to light.

It was the first time I'd ever been in a luxury hotel. The receptionist looked as though he recognized me, he'd probably seen me walking down Cañada. You might say hello one day, comrade. We went up. He opened the door for me and then took a couple of bottles of porter out of the refrigerator, thus beginning my weakness for the beer that continues to this day. He opened the curtains and the city stretched out below us. The same hostile, dirty city I walked every night glowed when seen from on high. From the right angle, I thought, Córdoba looks like it's worth something.

He asked me if I had much time and I answered that time depended on money, forgive me for saying so but that's life. He laughed and so did I, but I didn't know how to cover my awkwardness. In the gap left by the subsequent silence, he looked at me and said: "You're angry. You're full of anger."

He politely asked me to take off my clothes and to lie face down on the rug. Then he sat on my rump and started to massage my back. My eyes filled with tears. It was true, so true that it made me angry: with the world, my parents, my current love interest, my profession, life, the neighborhood where I lived, politicians, heaven and hell. But bringing it to the surface like that broke me. It's not a wild leap to guess that a twenty-two-year-old travesti prostituting herself on a summer's night by a funeral home might be angry, or angry with her lot in life. But it was the first time that a john had given me a massage. And neither had one ever articulated my pain before. It was my resentment that hurt the most. It enraged me so that I transmuted everything: relief into tension, courtesy into rudeness, openness into falsehoods, pain into anger.

When he was done with his massage, he lay down next to me and told me that he'd been hired to work in Córdoba by the provincial government but that the next day he was going to Buenos Aires because he needed to do some tests. He'd been undergoing tests for five months but the doctors hadn't found anything.

I didn't ask any questions, I just let him speak. Interpreting my silence as an invitation to share more, he told me that they'd found some blots on his lungs and he was sure that it was cancer. He wasn't sad when he said it, he even smiled a little.

"I've smoked since I was fourteen so I can't say that it seems unfair."

I didn't know how to reply to his confession, I was still young, I didn't understand. Death was a concept I couldn't get my head around. All I knew was how to get through the day and avoid the dangers that stalked me at every turn. I didn't yet know that death had been with me since I was born, that she had my name tattooed on her forehead, that she holds my hand at night, sits down to eat with me, that we breathe in unison.

While part of me listened to what he was saying, another felt immortal and regarded him without empathy. It seemed as though he took a degree of pleasure in knowing that his days were numbered, like he was playing at doing everything for the last time. It also seemed as though he trusted me. I asked him if he'd ever been with a travesti before and he said he hadn't. I told him it's like being bitten by a vampire: you don't go back.

A few minutes later we were fucking, a little clumsily, and all the while I was thinking, *He's going to die, he's going to die,* fucking him like I was afraid I was going to break him. But I soon welcomed him into my body, like a stranger eager to explore my territory.

After the orgasm, he collapsed, gasping for breath. A little while later he told me that he had a wife. He let some more time go by before saying that she was a young woman and it bothered him to dump all this on her. They didn't have children. I was a little upset by the confession. It was a jealous impulse, I knew that, because for some of the night I'd had him all to myself. But deep down, in the basement of this story, there was nothing for me. Just my body, which I sold so I could live as a woman. I checked the time and saw that dawn was still some ways off, but I wanted to get back home, just then I wanted to be between the four shoddily painted walls of my room, with its family photos glued to the walls.

We said goodbye as though we'd never said what we'd said or felt what we'd felt. I asked him if I could just walk out the front door. He laughed and said of course, just walk out naturally. I nodded to the concierge as I passed by. When I got to the corner, I looked up to try to find his window, but all the lights on his floor were off.

———

AUNTIE ENCARNA peered out through the blinds at the street. For a few days now the same white car had been parking as close as it could to her house and sitting there for hours with two men inside. They looked as though they were watching the windows. The plants were now so overgrown that they'd spread right across the roof and were spilling over the front of the house, covering it with a thick blanket of leaves that barely allowed in any light. Just enough to write poetry by. Auntie Encarna was forced to deal with the harassment almost alone. None of us was there to help her. We didn't know what was going on. Twinkle had stopped talking and his mother limited herself to saying what she needed from the supermarket: it was all the help she'd accept, letting us do her grocery shopping. When we were allowed in we saw the boy whittling figures of all the animals we'd been: bird women, she-wolves, sad women, brave women, a whole mythology carved in figurines the boy created in his isolation. In Auntie Encarna's room we caught a glimpse of her chest lying open with her jewels in plain sight.

We all knew either the real or fictitious story behind each of the pieces, some of which had been given to Auntie by colonels and monsignors: rings that had been on the pope's fingers, diamonds embedded in white gold snakes, emeralds, rubies. We'd all seen them. And we'd also all seen the neighbors, talking to one another, pointing out the house of sin. Encarna knew they were coming for her. For her and the boy. Along with all his blessings, Twinkle brought with him the metallic taste of fear. Ever since the boy came into her life,

Auntie Encarna had known what fear was. She could taste it on her tongue.

I MET AUNTIE MARA just when, like Mamma Roma, I'd said goodbye, I'm going, and abandoned my old haunts after witnessing a pair of travestis slash each other up during a scuffle in which my face got spattered with blood. Having watched them almost kill each other over a car cruising for a pickup, I decided I wouldn't go back to the Park again. Auntie Mara lived two blocks over from me. I often saw her in the supermarket, at the grocery store, sometimes in the telephone booths on Colón and Mendoza. We acknowledged one another. Sometimes she smiled at me. Sometimes, inexplicably, she was dressed as a man in a checked shirt with her dancing girl's mane pulled back in a ponytail and the shapeless jeans we all wear sometimes, like we're airline passengers in transit. When she was dressed like that, as a man, she didn't smile at me. When she was Auntie Mara, she gave me a knowing look, full of love.

One night when business was slow, I went out looking for tricks and saw her in action for the first time. Auntie Mara on acrylic heels that made her look as though she were floating, like those virgins who levitate, powered by their own beauty. She was adjusting her clothes after getting out of a car that was already pulling away, to which she waved with a giant paw so white and polished that it looked like marble. When she saw me, she turned the gesture into a fraternal greeting, which she seasoned with a "Come over here, you fairy!" that had me running over to her like a moth to a flame, my heart in my mouth at the prospect that she'd slit my face open for intruding on her patch. But she was different from the others, starting with her perfume. We all thought that we set ourselves apart with our perfume and travestis at the time liked sweet flavors with a little citrus. But no one smelled like Auntie Mara. When I got to her she asked if I'd like to have a coffee with her but I said I didn't have any money.

"Oh, a poor fairy! Then you're coming home for a coffee. Did you see the car that pulled away just now? Ever been with him? He pays to stroke. I lie back and he shoves his hand under my clothes. Then he pays and leaves. He makes me feel like a queen." She didn't have to try very hard to convince me to call it a day, and we walked to her house. On the way she told me that she knew all about me. She saw me sometimes at El Ojo Bizarro, a unique place we'll miss forever. She knew where I worked, where I came from, the name on my ID, and what I studied. Back then, our lovers went from travesti to travesti, spreading gossip: they would pass on our secrets before leaving us.

Auntie Mara's house was pink, just like Auntie Encarna's. Against the wall was an aquarium containing a pair of enormous creatures waggling their tails and impossibly colored fins. She spoke to them as she came in as though she expected them to answer back. We were in the room where she entertained her johns, which had air conditioning and a lava lamp. Mara said that one should never sleep in the same bed where they fuck clients. I thought that was extremely classy, worthy of a woman who speaks to fish. A mirror hung from one of the walls so that johns could see themselves hugging her and know that it wasn't a hallucination. Then she showed me the bedroom where she slept. That was when Auntie Mara grew to her full height in my eyes: the kitchen at the back, a potted plant on top of the fridge, some horrible porcelain figures on the windowsill, and a lace tablecloth with artificial flowers in the center along with a teapot in a crochet warmer. Auntie Mara gave me a choice between instant coffee and flavored tea. I chose coffee and she made it, served it, and while it was cooling wrote something down in a notebook. She looked up and told me it was her customer log. She entered them under their name or nickname or, if she didn't have either, she'd mention a physical characteristic or the make and color of their car. Next she'd note down how much they'd paid and the gifts from those who didn't pay in cash: a bottle of wine, a knickknack or ornament. Once she got a clock.

That appeared in a different notebook in which she recorded her lovers: an insane chronicle of all the men with whom she'd slept for free, for whom she had suffered. She didn't show me that one, but she did the other. At the end of each month she totted up the money she'd made and wrote it down. The figures were unbelievable. She was almost rich. But Auntie Mara found it hard to save anything because she had three children from a former life.

She was the embodiment of hospitality. I'm certain that was exactly what all her johns and lovers felt. Auntie Mara was a woman who'd invented her own rules, a framework consisting of small but genuine gestures designed to make the person she was with feel comfortable. She'd made it into an art form and dedicated herself to it. The fish, the lava lamp, the leopard-skin cushions, the bed for johns and cot for lovers. And there was also that other life as a man, the life we travestis try to consign to the past, freeze, or destroy once we've given it up. I'll never understand how she managed to live with one foot in each realm.

Auntie Mara was a part of our country's history, the happy, pornographic story of a country where bold men worked the land and the grandchildren of immigrants populated it, all of whom, the foreigners, the Blacks, the Indians, and the mestizos, to a man, would have been burned at the stake for sleeping with a travesti. Auntie Mara had kept a record of all those who had once, twice, or more, out of desperation, curiosity, or secret yearning, given themselves to a travesti body. She had a full chronicle of those occasions and expected them all to come back to her travesti pagoda with the confidence of someone who knows that for certain people it's easier to die than change.

I WAS NEARBY Auntie Encarna's house and decided to ring her doorbell. It had been almost seven months since I'd last seen her. I had been going through a rough time, really rough: my mother got sick and needed an operation. A couple of johns had robbed me, pretending to be desperate for sex, that old ruse. They'd choked me until I passed out and then stolen everything they thought looked valuable, the tacky things a woman like me is able to accumulate in her life. But no, that wasn't it. I hadn't seen her in seven months because I was pissed. Encarna never called me, not even to see how my recovery was going. I heard through the grapevine that the police were turning up at her house at all hours and the neighbors were throwing all kinds of things into her patio. The walls were covered with graffiti and the door was scorched from a couple of arson attempts. The other travestis living there had fled in panic after being systematically harassed every time they opened the door.

But Auntie Encarna's problems had been eclipsed in our minds by a wave of travesti murders. Every time the newspapers reported a new crime, the bastards used the victim's male name. The term travesti was condemnation in itself. The intention was to make us pay with every last drop of blood we had. They didn't want any of us to survive. One was stoned to death. Another was burned alive, like a witch: she had gas poured over her and was set alight by the side of the road. More and more disappeared. There was a monster out there, a monster who fed on travestis. We were just disappearing overnight. The fewer ties between us, the easier it was to make us disappear. News traveled fast. We heard about each new rape, the latest victim, almost immediately. It was a dangerous world. I was heading for Auntie Encarna's door because I'd heard that she'd stopped taking the boy to school after he had been subjected to the worst kind of bullying you can think of. Twinkle had been silent in the face of countless injustices. He endured a terrifying amount of abuse. And the poor little saint never complained, he never told his mother what was going on at school. One day he came home with his fingers swollen and purple, he couldn't wrap them around a mug. Some of the boys at school had jammed them in a door.

"Why?" Auntie Encarna asked.

"Because I'm your son," Twinkle answered.

Auntie Encarna asked him if he wanted to keep going to school or whether he'd rather have private classes at home. Twinkle didn't answer so she decided for him. She put up signs on lampposts around the neighborhood: LOVING AND OPEN-MINDED TUTOR REQUIRED. But the few who did ring the doorbell were scared off by the beard and lumpy breasts of their potential employer.

The only one who understood, the only witness, was Maria, the caged bird, forgotten in her silver prison. She was entirely dependent on the boy; he was the only one who remembered to feed her. Sometimes weeks might go by without an incident but then there'd be a bottle smashed against the door or a plant pot filled with shit would crash into the patio, or they'd get an anonymous phone call at four in the morning. Our mother stayed locked up in her house like a nun in cloisters. We forgot about her, our attention focused on staying alive and waiting for things to change. The only ones to remember her were those who'd managed to escape overseas. They sent her postcards describing the "normal" lives they led, earning euros from inoffensive truckers by the side of the road in anonymous small towns. Here, in contrast, the panic made us make bad decisions and choose the wrong johns.

———

"YOU'RE GOING TO END UP in a ditch," my father had once said to me from the head of the table.

"You have a right to be happy," said Auntie Encarna from her easy chair in the patio. "You have every opportunity to be happy."

And spurred by those memories I walked back along streets that we once thought of as ours. I went down Obispo Salguero, but the area didn't seem so neglected any more, especially when it became Calle Salta. There were more open businesses, people walking dogs in the street. From afar I saw that a black glass building had been built right opposite Auntie Encarna's house. Its windows reflected the jungle that had grown over the roof of the travesti boardinghouse. It stood out in the neighborhood like a fortress made of thickly entwined branches and leaves garrisoned by birds and butterflies. A tough green moss had grown on the walls to the street so thick you couldn't pull it off with your bare hands. Ferocious street curs, the offspring of the dogs that had belonged to our bum sister, roamed around the entrance in silence or lay in front of the door. People said that it was impossible to get rid of them. Sometimes they sent municipal employees dressed like yellow astronauts to try to capture them or scare them off. The neighbors had tried to poison and electrocute them but these dogs wouldn't be fooled. However people came at them, they were already expecting it and knew how to defend themselves. Underneath the decay, the house was still pink. A hopeful pink, an obvious pink, our pink, an impossible, unreal pink.

I was a block and a half away when I saw the red and green lights flashing savagely at Auntie Encarna's door. A crowd had formed, the street was blocked to traffic, sirens could be heard. I quickened my pace. In my purse I had a little figurine of the Difunta Correa and some cookies, the most expensive I could find at the supermarket. I made my way through the massed people, local residents were appearing in doors and windows, some spying through blinds, some from their balconies.

The commotion was focused on our mother's house. The dogs had gone nuts, keeping gawkers and the police at bay, barking up at the windows where the neighbors hurled down insults at them. They were enraged, the hair on their backs was standing on end, as many as thirty bitches of every size and shade. I elbowed myself forward and came across Little Girl, who was sobbing like a waterworks. She hugged me, so upset she couldn't speak. When I saw the ambulance and fire truck, I tried to shrug her off. "Faggots! Murderers!" someone shouted from a window or balcony. The police had arrested a travesti I didn't know. She was naked under her robe. I shouted for them to please at least give her time to get dressed, it was cold, but no one listened to me. They shoved her into the police car, hitting her head against the roof. I saw the Headless Men watching on from a prudent distance, one of them was talking to a pair of policewomen whose role was unclear. Little by little I managed to get through and into the house. A fireman stopped me with a hand against my chest, my foam chest, the chest that feels everything that's wrong with this goddamn country. "You can't be here, sir," he said. I let the insult pass and asked what happened, saying I was a friend of the owner. The fireman told me that Auntie Encarna had turned on the gas and killed herself along with Twinkle. From where I stood I could see our mother's enormous feet in her room. She looked like she was asleep in bed, lying face down. Not even in death did they show any respect for our mother, our whore mother whom we were unable to save. The fireman told me that the room had been sealed from inside with rags shoved in the cracks under the door and windows. They were going to file it as a murder-suicide. "She's very welcome to kill herself, but taking the kid along with her, that's unforgivable," said the fireman. I told him that there were jewels in Encarna's bedroom and asked who had been in charge of the operation. The fireman got tense and then giggled nervously, saying no jewels had been found.

I looked in the kitchen and saw Maria the Bird in her cage, throwing herself crazily against the bars. I tried to go to rescue her but the fireman started to get rough. Then we were stopped in our tracks by a bloodcurdling, deafening scream and I saw a set of curved leopard-skin nails and then an arm covered in fish-scale bracelets. "What's that?" the fireman mumbled in shock.

It was our medicine woman, La Machi, who had the power to stun policemen, firemen, nurses, and gawkers all at once. La Machi walked between them with her hand held high, no one got in her way, and she opened Maria's cage. She flew off clumsily, like a bat, and perched on the highest branch in the patio, above the roof. Behind the medicine woman, the travestis filed in silently. La Machi led those closest to her into the bedroom and we stood there, taking in the scene: the boy lying on his side next to his mother. They died face to face, looking into each other's eyes. They died wisely, knowing they could bear no further humiliation. Our mother and her adored son. What else was there to say? La Machi knelt down by the bed and began to sing in tongues, puffing on her cigar, blowing smoke over the bodies until they were enveloped in a cloud. Outside, not a sound could be heard. When the ritual was over she raised her head and sniffed the air. "The jewels are still in the house," she said. "Go look." In silence, still moved by the ceremony, the travestis began to search the house and vegetation. The activity seemed to rouse the police and firemen from their stupor, they tried to stop us but couldn't move. From the back of the house, one of the girls shouted that she'd found them. Then La Machi gave the order to leave and we trooped outside in silence. Maria the Bird flew down into my purse and I let her settle in there.

Outside, everyone was crying: the gawkers who just a few moments before had been shouting insults at us as well as the few people who knew and liked us, everyone had fallen under the spell of grief. As we walked away we saw the Headless Men following us at a distance. The dogs brought up the rear of the funeral procession, guarding our backs. We were headed to the Park. La Machi clicked her fingers and chanted and we answered in unison, but the city didn't hear us, it had already forgotten who we were. Night fell as we said goodbye to our mother. It was very cold. A couple of rag-and-bone men halted their carts to allow us to pass and waved us goodbye.

When we got to the Park, the flasks and cigarettes came out and we started to share stories about how we'd met our mother, what she'd done for each of us, she was a goddess with feet of clay and a boxer's fists. One of the youngest started to play music on her cell phone and we all danced to accompany Auntie Encarna and Twinkle in Her Eye's ascent into travesti heaven. If they lost their way, they only had to listen out for us. The dogs ran around between our legs, almost knocking us over. Anonymous, transparent, godmothers to a boy found in a ditch and raised by travestis, the only ones who knew the secret about the Difunta Correa's child. We, the forgotten ones, no longer had a name. It was as though we'd never been there at all.

CAMILA SOSA VILLADA was born in 1982 in La Falda (Córdoba, Argentina). She is a writer, actress, and singer, and previously earned a living as a sex worker, street vendor, and hourly maid. She holds degrees in communication and theater from the National University of Córdoba. Her play *Carnes tolendas, retrato escénico de un travesti* was selected for the 2010 National Theater Festival held in La Plata. Her first novel, *Bad Girls*, won the Premio Sor Juana Inés de la Cruz and the Grand Prix de l'Héroïne Madame Figaro and will be translated into six languages.

KIT MAUDE is a translator based in Buenos Aires. He has translated dozens of classic and contemporary Latin American writers such as Armonía Somers, Jorge Luis Borges, Lolita Copacabana, and Ariel Magnus for a wide array of publications and writes reviews and criticism for several outlets in Spanish and English including the *Times Literary Supplement*, *Revista Ñ* and *Otra Parte*.